Say Goodnight, Gracie

Say Goodnight, Gracie

JULIE REECE DEAVER

HarperTrophy®
A Division of HarperCollinsPublishers

PICK YOURSELF UP by Dorothy Fields and
Jerome Kern. Copyright © by T.B. Harms Company.
Copyright renewed (c/o The Welk Music Group,
Santa Monica, CA, 90401) International Copyright
Secured. All rights reserved. Used by Permission.

Say Goodnight, Gracie

Library of Congress Cataloging-in-Publication Data
Deaver, Julie Reece.
   Say goodnight, Gracie.
   "A Charlotte Zolotow book."
   Summary: When a car accident kills her best friend
Jimmy, with whom she has shared everything from
childhood escapades to breaking into the professional
theater scene in Chicago, seventeen-year-old Morgan
must find her own way of coping with his death.
   [Death—Fiction.   2. Friendship—Fiction.
3. Actors and actresses—Fiction.   4. Chicago (Ill.)—
Fiction]   I. Title.
PZ7.D3524Say   1988   [Fic]   87-45278
ISBN 0-06-021418-X
ISBN 0-06-021419-8 (lib. bdg.)
ISBN 0-06-447007-5 (pbk.)

for my brother, Jeff, who is a little like Jimmy,
and grandmother, Ethel May Rider,
and to the memory of my parents, Danny Deaver
and Dee Rider Deaver

My thanks to these writers and professionals
who have helped and encouraged me:

Babette Rosmond
Treva Silverman
Nancy Geller

Say Goodnight, Gracie

Part One

1

There are friends, I think, we can't imagine living without. People who are sisters to us, or brothers. Jimmy was one of those. I never thought I might have to go through life without him. I never thought he might be killed by a drunken driver or anything else. Who thinks about things like that when you're seventeen? If I had known ahead of time what was going to happen to him, I would have gone crazy. I guess I *did* go a little crazy. My Aunt Lo, who's a hospital psychiatrist, says grief travels a certain route—that if you could plot it out on a map you'd have a line that twists and weaves and eventually ends up near the point of departure. I say "near" because although you may survive the grief, you won't ever be exactly the same. It took me a long time to learn that, and sometimes the whole experience comes back on me and I have to learn it all over again.

"Hey, Morgan," I remember Jimmy saying. "Watch!" It was the summer we were ten. The summer he discovered Fred Astaire and fell in love with dancing. (In

3

fact, by the time we were fifteen he was as tall and lanky as Astaire and was dancing professionally at the local dinner theater.)

"Come on," he'd say. "Dance with me."

"I'm reading." I'd be sitting on the Woolfs' porch swing, and Jimmy would take the book from me and grab my hands and pull me to my feet. "But I can't *dance*," I'd say.

"You have to," Jimmy would answer. "*Somebody has to be Ginger Rogers. . . .*" He would have memorized one of their routines from an old movie on TV, and while he did all the actual dancing, I remember whirling around and around the porch those hot summer days so long ago and never wanting to stop.

When I think about it now, I realize that Jimmy and I started out our lives as friends. Our mothers had been high school friends who happened to reacquaint in the maternity wing of Geneva Hospital the week we were born. Because of our mothers, who were a bit fanatical about recording the history of our childhood with pictures, there are lots of photographs of Jimmy and me. The last time Jimmy and I looked through the album was an end-of-summer day, a day hot enough to melt rock, and we were in the kitchen trying to cool down with iced coffee. The rest of the house was jumping with music and noise and postadolescent energy. Besides friends and neighbors, Jimmy's folks and my aunt were there. I was feeling sentimental that day, so

I dragged out the album and made him look through it.

"Ah, just what I've always wanted to do," he said. "Trip down memory lane."

But I made him look anyway. One of the first pictures in the album was taken of Jimmy and me when we were just a few days old.

"You were pretty cute," he said. "But I had more hair."

"Big deal. Two strands more."

"Two more's a lot more, Hackett."

Other pictures, carefully labeled by our mothers, show the evolution of our friendship: Jimmy and Morgan's third-birthday party (Jimmy smearing cake into Morgan's hair, very touching), Jimmy and Morgan's first day of school (I wouldn't go into the classroom unless he was holding my hand), the last day of summer camp, Jimmy and Morgan's graduation from junior high (*he* graduated with honors, *I* flunked gym), Jimmy and Morgan in his secondhand MG, Jimmy and Morgan turn seventeen. This last picture, one of my favorites, was taken in Jimmy's backyard. In it we have our arms casually draped around each other's shoulders, which pretty much shows what our relationship was like. We never looked at each other as the objects of romantic love. I liked it that way. So did Jimmy. "What we have is better," he said once. "Lovers come and go, but friends go on and on."

"Hey, Hackett," Jimmy said. "You're out of coffee."

5

I looked at him. He was holding the coffeepot, and I realized he hadn't even bothered with the last few pages of the album.

"Make some more then!" I said.

"Now, now . . . don't look at me like that, Morgan. You know what those pictures do to me. It's all I can do to hold back the tears." I knew part of him was kidding, but part of what he had said was true. Of the two of us, I would classify him as more open with his feelings and more sentimental.

"Oh, make your coffee," I said. "But that's the last time I go down memory lane or anyplace else with you."

"We're going into the Loop tomorrow, aren't we? As usual?"

"I guess so," I said. Three times a week after school Jimmy and I caught the 3:25 into the city. Jimmy went to a dance class in the Loop, and I went to an acting workshop at Second City, which is an improvisational theater in the Old Town section of Chicago.

"Have you seen your aunt yet?" Jimmy asked. "She looks exceptionally entrancing today."

"I think she's in love again." I slammed the album shut and stood up and looked at my reflection in the window. "You know what I'm going to have her do this afternoon? Pierce my ears."

"You?"

"Yeah. What do you think?"

"*You?*"

6

"Why not?"

"You hate needles. You hate blood. You even get squeamish watching Bactine commercials."

"I just wanted to know what you thought, okay? Spare me the diatribe."

"You want to know what I think? I don't think you'll go through with it."

I frowned. Jimmy probably knew me better than anyone, which could be very annoying at times.

"Five bucks," I said. "Five bucks says I go through with it."

"Why not ten?"

"Fine. Ten." I cleared my throat. "Well. I'll just . . . I'll go find my aunt and see if she'll do it."

"You do that, Morgan. Tell her you're dying to have two more holes in your head."

I gave him a nasty smile and turned around and walked out into the living room.

I spotted my aunt right away. She was backed into a corner talking to a bunch of people. I knew exactly what was happening. Anytime we had a party, people drifted over to my aunt and asked for free psychiatric or medical advice. I thought that was pretty nervy until I realized I was about to do the same thing. She looked like she was drowning and waiting for someone to throw her a lifesaver, so I sort of waved to her, and that gave her an excuse to untangle herself from the crowd and come over to me.

"You," my aunt said, "are a doll. The next time

7

your parents throw one of these casual little get-togethers, I'm taking names and addresses and sending out bills."

"Aunt Lo, why do you come? This always happens—"

"Oh, well, your father's my big brother, and I can't resist those twinkly eyes of his."

"What was the topic of the day?"

"Gall bladders."

"Yuchh," I said. "Oh, Aunt Lo, here comes Mrs. Johnson. She has a bad back *and* a bad marriage—"

"Good God, I'll be here all night. Let's get out of here."

We ended up in the kitchen. Jimmy was just pouring coffee into glasses filled with cracked ice.

"Dr. Hackett," Jimmy said, "has she asked you yet?"

"Asked me what?"

"Morgan wants her ears pierced. Preferably now. Before she loses her nerve."

My aunt looked at me. "Are you sure about this?"

"I'm sure. Will you do it? Now?"

"Don't you remember what happened when I gave you that tetanus shot last year? You took one look at the needle and almost passed out—"

"I did not!"

"You did," Jimmy said. "I was there."

"Okay, that was last year! That was *last* year, all right? Maybe I've changed since then!" I looked at my aunt. "Will you do it?"

"Honey, you'll have to get earrings, and I don't have any surgical needles in my bag—"

"*Surgical needles?*" This was starting to sound more complicated than I'd thought.

"I'll tell you what," my aunt said. "You're coming into the city tomorrow, aren't you? Why don't you drop by the hospital around six and we'll do it then, okay?"

"Uh, okay," I said. I didn't know if I'd still have my nerve the next day: I didn't like hospitals, and I especially didn't like the idea of a "surgical needle," which I pictured as very long and very sharp.

"Don't look so worried," my aunt said. "I've been a doctor for twelve years, and I've never heard of anyone dying from having her ears pierced."

"There's always a first time," I said.

Jimmy handed my aunt a glass of coffee. "Morgan always looks on the bright side."

There was a quiet knock on the kitchen door, and Mrs. Johnson opened it and peeked in. "Oh, Dr. Hackett, there you are! I wonder if I could talk to you a moment—I promise not to take up too much of your time. . . ."

"That's what they all say," my aunt whispered. Jimmy and I looked at each other and smiled, and as Mrs. Johnson dragged her out of the kitchen, my aunt called back: "Don't forget the earrings!"

9

2

Not only did I forget the earrings, I forgot my sweater, purse, and train ticket, too. The problem was my last class of the day. Glenbard West was this beautiful castlelike structure some sadist built on the top of a very steep hill. It even had a brick turret, the fifth floor, where I took art each day. As soon as the bell sounded, I had seven minutes—just seven—to dash down five flights of stairs, go to my locker, and race down the street to the station in time to catch the 3:25. Usually I made it with a couple of minutes to spare, but not this time. This time I barely had a foot on the train before it started moving. Jimmy was waiting for me in the next-to-the-last car.

"I was watching you," he said. "You should go out for track."

I wanted to say something smart back to him, something sarcastic and witty and rude, but I had a terrible stitch in my side, and it was all I could do to collapse onto the seat facing him. He leaned back in his seat and stretched out his long legs and plopped his feet up beside me.

"Hey, the conductor's coming," I said. "Move your feet."

"These feet are going to be famous someday."

"Well, they're not now, so move them." He pulled his feet down and handed the conductor his ticket. That's when I discovered I'd forgotten mine. I reached for my purse and it wasn't there.

"Jimmy!" I whispered. "I left my purse at school!"

"Ticket, please," the conductor said.

"I don't have one," I said. "I mean, I forgot it. My friend will buy me another one." The conductor and I both waited for Jimmy, who was busy staring out the window.

"Jimmy!" I gave him a little kick. "I forgot my ticket! You've got to buy me another one!"

He looked at me blankly. "Are you talking to me?"

"Yes, I'm talking to you! Of *course* I'm talking to you! I told the conductor you'd pay for my ticket—"

"Why should I pay for your ticket? I've never even *seen* you before—"

"Jimmy, this isn't funny!"

"Look, kids," the conductor said, "is this some kind of initiation or something? Because if the young lady here doesn't buy a ticket, off she goes at the next stop—"

"I guess you'll be walking into the city, then," Jimmy said.

I gave him one of my dirtiest looks. "Jimmy Woolf . . . do you realize how close to death you are right now?"

"Oh, all right," he said, reaching for his wallet.

After he paid the conductor, I said, "Why do you *do* that?!"

"Do what?"

"You know what! Act weird!"

"Well, Morgan . . . you try your best to go through life unnoticed. I try my best not only to be noticed, but to be remembered, too."

"Well, I'm sure the conductor will never forget you," I said. "I know *I* won't."

When we got into the station, Jimmy gave me cab fare and walked me out onto Canal Street to the taxi stand.

"I'll meet you in front of Field's in about an hour," I said. "Dance good."

"Don't I always?"

Walking into the theater gave me chills—the good kind. I knew I was feeling the ghosts of a lot of acting heavyweights who'd been at Second City before me: Shelley Long, Bill Murray, Robert Klein, John Belushi. At one time or another they'd all started out here, standing on the same stage I was standing on now.

"Okay," the director said. "Instead of starting with

improvisations today, I thought we'd try something a little different. . . . Everybody grab a chair and arrange yourselves in a semicircle, like an orchestra does." We all got settled onstage. I thought maybe we were going to pantomime musicians. "Instead of musical instruments, you'll each be playing an emotion." And he assigned each of us an emotion: fear, happiness, anger, sorrow.

"How about it, Morgan?" he said. "Think you can handle paranoia?"

"I'll try anything once," I said.

"Okay, then . . . when I point to you I want you to 'play' paranoia. Got it?"

I nodded. I kept my eyes glued to the director. He raised his arms and started waving them like a berserk Leonard Bernstein. When he pointed to me I jumped up. Knocked my chair over. I ran across the stage and crouched in a corner. I tried to dredge up some scary experience I could be paranoid about, and I suddenly remembered my upcoming ear piercing.

"You're really loosening up, Morgan," the director said. "That's about the best acting you've done since you've been here."

I pictured one of those surgical needles my aunt had talked about the day before, and I shuddered.

"Who's acting?" I said.

Jimmy was waiting for me in front of Field's. I got out of the cab, and before I even had a chance to pay the driver, he grabbed me around the waist and started swinging me in the air.

"Jimmy Woolf, are you crazy?" I hollered. "Put me down!"

"Morgan," he said, setting me on my feet. "Isn't this a beautiful day! Isn't this a wonderful city! Do you know how *pretty* you are?!"

"Why don't you cheer up?" I said. I paid the driver, who was giving us a very strange look; then I turned back to Jimmy and took a good long look at him. He was positively beaming. "All right," I said. "I know you want me to ask. What happened? Did you break some sort of dancing record or something? I know. The greatest number of pirouettes ever turned in a single afternoon, right?"

"Much better," he said. "My teacher got me an audition for *Oklahoma!*"

"You're kidding!"

"It's not just a dinner-theater show. It's going to be right here. Downtown. They're casting the principals out of New York and the dancers out of Chicago. Isn't that great? After it plays at the Shubert, it's going on the road—"

"When do you try out?"

"The first audition is this Friday. If they like what I do, I get a callback and audition again. My teacher seems to think I have a shot at it."

"Of course you do," I said. "Nobody dances as good as you."

"Come on. Let's go to the hospital and tell your aunt."

"Jimmy, wait—let's just get something to eat and go home. My earrings are in the purse I left at school, so there's no point in going all the way over to the hospital—"

"Aha! You know *why* you forgot your earrings, don't you?"

"Because I was hurrying—"

"Because your subconscious is afraid of having its ears pierced."

"Jimmy, do you ever get the feeling we're living in an old black-and-white rerun of *The Burns and Allen Show*? Only just once *I'd* like the chance to be Gracie, and you can be George Burns and play straight man."

"You hate anything medical. So you conveniently forget about the earrings, and then you don't have to face any needles."

"That's the dumbest thing I've ever heard."

"It isn't dumb. Ask your aunt."

"I will. But the fact remains: If I haven't got any earrings, I can't have my ears pierced, can I?"

He looked at his watch. "I think we have time to go into Field's and make a purchase."

Ever since I was a little kid I've loved Marshall Field's. My grandmother says *her* grandmother used to shop here, and whenever I walk into the store, I like to think

I'm wandering around the same counters my great-great-grandmother once did.

"See anything you like?" Jimmy asked.

"Do you know how expensive some of this stuff is?"

"So?"

"Look, can't we just forget about this and go home?"

"No, we cannot."

"But you can't afford—"

"Shut up, Hackett." He pointed to some beautiful gold heart-shaped earrings in a showcase. "How about these? Do you like these?"

"How much are they?"

"Do you *like* them?"

"How much *are* they?"

"Miss?" Jimmy said to the salesclerk. "We'd like these earrings, please."

"Cash or charge?"

"Cash."

"Let's see . . . that's thirty-seven fifty plus tax—"

"Jimmy!" I said. "I will not allow you to spend that much money on me!"

"I want to do this. When you're a famous actress, I'll be able to say, 'I bought her her first pair of earrings.' You can wear them to the Academy Awards."

"I can't let you do this."

"Didn't anyone ever tell you just to smile and say thank you?"

"I don't want you to spend all your money on me! I don't want—"

He ran his fingers through his hair and sighed. "Just say goodnight, Gracie."

"Goodnight, Gracie," I said.

When we got to the hospital it was around dinner-time, so there wasn't much traffic in the halls. My aunt's floor was practically deserted, and the only person at the nurses' station was a student nurse, a girl who looked just a year or two older than us.

"Hey," Jimmy whispered. "Do you know her?"

"No," I said. "I've never seen her before."

"Good. Wait here."

"Why? What are you going to do?"

"You'll see."

I grabbed his arm. "Jimmy, you're going to do something crazy, aren't you? You're going to go up to that girl and do something crazy and embarrass me—"

"Oh, come on. I'm just going to have a little fun—"

"*Fun?* This is the psychiatric floor! If you start acting weird around here, they'll lock you up!"

"Excuse me," the girl called from the desk. "Can I help you?"

"Yes," Jimmy said. He walked over to the counter and talked to her in a low voice: "You see that girl I'm with?"

The student nurse looked at me and nodded.

"She's a patient here," Jimmy said. "This morning while no one was looking, she sneaked out. I found her down on State Street talking to herself."

17

"Oh my God," I said.

"I don't know how that *happened*," the girl said. "Who's her doctor?"

"Dr. Hackett," Jimmy said.

"She is not my doctor!" I yelled.

Jimmy leaned closer to the girl. "She's hysterical—"

"I see," the girl said.

"You *don't* see!" I said. "Look, my friend here has a warped sense of humor. Dr. Hackett's expecting me. She's going to pierce my ears—"

The student nurse just stared at me. "Your *psychiatrist* is going to pierce your ears?"

"She's not my psychiatrist! She's my aunt!"

"Uh, of course she is," the girl said. "I'll go get her. Don't go anywhere." She went off down the hall, and Jimmy laughed and leaned back against the counter.

"Don't forget the straitjacket!" he called after her.

"God, what's the *matter* with you?"

"Morgan . . . you take things entirely too seriously. You've got to lighten up a little." He jammed his fingers into my side and started tickling me.

"Stop it!" I started laughing. I tried to tickle him back, but he kept out of reach so effectively that by the time my aunt and the student nurse appeared, Jimmy was the one in control and I was the one doubled over and laughing like a hyena. My aunt stood there quietly, her arms folded over her white coat.

"Dr. Hackett," Jimmy said, "you look beautiful. Like a Freudian bird in a guilted cage." (My aunt really is very pretty, but she has this sharp-eyed intelligent look that keeps her from being beautiful. I have this feeling when I look at her that there are about a million things going on in her head all at once.)

"Rosalie," said my aunt. "This is my niece, Morgan, and Jimmy here is a friend of hers. I wouldn't want to swear to it, of course, but I'm reasonably sure neither of them is crazy. All right, you two," she said, "follow me."

"Catch you later, Rosalie," Jimmy said.

"Uh-huh," Rosalie answered.

We followed my aunt down the hall, and she opened the door to her office. "Why don't you go on inside," she said. "I'll get the equipment and be right back, okay?"

I followed Jimmy into the office. "She said 'equipment,' " I whispered. "But she meant 'needles.' "

"What did you *think* she was going to use to pierce your ears?" Jimmy asked. "Polo mallets?"

My aunt's office didn't look like what you'd think a psychiatrist's office would look like: It was small and sunny and comfortable. There was a lot of original artwork on the walls. Some of it my father had painted. He's a professional artist and he paints these terrific scenes of things within his everyday grasp: old buildings around Glen Ellyn, people shopping in the village, front porches of our neighbors' homes.

"When did your dad do this one?" Jimmy asked. He

was looking at a painting my father had just finished of the antique horse trough on Main Street.

"It's from his new collection."

"Hey, doesn't your father ever get a little nervous that one of your aunt's wacko patients might walk off with some of his valuable artwork?"

"They're not wacko, Jimmy. Just a little disturbed. Like you."

He walked over to the bookcase, where there was a coffeepot and a stack of Styrofoam cups. "You want some coffee?" he asked.

"Uh, no . . . I'm jumpy enough."

"Maybe your aunt'll give you a general anesthetic—"

"Don't be stupid," I said. I sat down on the couch. "You don't have to stick around if you don't want to."

"Who says I don't want to? You don't think I'd let you go through major surgery alone, do you?"

I tried not to smile. I didn't want him to think I needed him, but I was glad he was there. He was always there when I needed him.

My aunt came in with her hands crammed full of medical-looking things.

"Don't do anything too drastic, Dr. Hackett," Jimmy said. "A frontal lobotomy will do just fine."

My aunt smiled and set her equipment on the bookcase. "It's not going to be as bad as you think," she said, touching my face. "Do you have your earrings?" I took the earrings out of the bag and handed them to

20

her. Jimmy sat down on the edge of my aunt's desk and took a packet of peanuts out of his jacket pocket and started munching them.

"How can you sit there eating *peanuts*?" I asked.

He looked at me. "What do you *want* me to do with them?"

"I can think of a suggestion or two," I said.

My aunt pulled my hair back with a rubber band. "Do you want to lie down or sit up?" she asked.

"I think I'll sit up," Jimmy said.

"Listen," I said, "you're not helping any. You're driving me nuts. Go talk to Rosalie or something." My aunt was cleaning off one ear with an alcohol-saturated cotton ball. "Aunt Lo, aren't you going to give me any Novocain or something?"

"I don't think you'll need it, honey." She pinched my earlobe, and it went numb. "This might hurt a little, but you can handle it. You're allowed to holler if you want to." Whenever my aunt does anything medical, she works very quickly. I never got a chance to see if the surgical needle was long or not. I never saw it at all. Before I knew what was happening, the first earring was in.

"You okay?" She handed me a wad of cotton. "Here. Hold this against your ear till the bleeding stops."

Jimmy leaned forward and watched with great curiosity. "What does it feel like?"

"Just peachy," I said. "You should try it sometime."

"Thanks. I live dangerously enough by carrying my ballet shoes through a tough neighborhood."

"Hold still now," my aunt said. "I'm almost through." I felt the second earring slip in. "There you go. . . . That wasn't too bad, was it?"

"I guess not."

She put her hand under my chin and looked at me. "You know what? I think you better lie down for a few minutes."

"I'm okay," I said.

"Just for a few minutes. Come on." My aunt has the kind of face where her eyes alone can do the smiling. I lay back on the couch and the three of us talked. I told her about being paranoid at Second City and Jimmy told her about his audition on Friday for *Oklahoma!*

"How long would you be on the road?" my aunt asked.

"Five months."

"Morgan will be lost without you—"

"Oh, for God's sake, I will not. The only difference I'll notice is I won't have somebody around razzing me twenty-four hours a day." I was about to say more, but my aunt very matter-of-factly took a cigarette out of her coat pocket and lit it. I couldn't believe my eyes. "Aunt Lo . . . when did you start smoking again?"

"Hmm," she said, taking a drag on her cigarette.

"Some days are better than other days. This is one of my weaker days."

"Don't you remember what you went through when you quit? You bit your fingernails—"

"I know."

"You bit *mine*!" I turned to Jimmy. "Do you *believe* this? And she's a doctor!"

"All right, sweetie, all right. Your point is well-taken." She ground out her cigarette in the ashtray, but not until she'd taken one last puff. "Okay? Let's see how you're doing." She took the cotton away and looked at my ears.

"Dr. Hackett," Jimmy said, "why don't we take you out to dinner? I've got enough money with me to swing an expensive meal as long as it's in the cafeteria."

"Yeah," I said. "Come on, Aunt Lo, it'll be fun."

"Thank you both, but I have a dinner date."

"Who is he?" I asked. "Anybody I know?"

"No—he's a doctor here. His name is Dan Petrie. He specializes in emergency medicine—"

"How long have you known him?" I asked. "Is it serious?"

"No," my aunt said. "It's *fun*."

"Ha ha. . . . No, really—are you just dating . . . or . . . well, *you* know—"

"That's right, Morgan," Jimmy said, "go right ahead and dig into your aunt's personal life—"

"She doesn't mind," I said. "What's he like?"

"Very nice and he laughs a lot," my aunt said. "I want you to meet him sometime."

"Why not now? Jimmy and I'll stick around and see if we approve of him."

"No, we won't," Jimmy said. "We're going to dinner, remember?"

"But I want to meet him," I said. "I'm not hungry."

My aunt smiled. "Yes, you are," she said. "You're starving."

3

Jimmy and I ditched school for his audition. Our teachers didn't seem to appreciate it when we missed class for things like auditions or workshops, so on days when we had something special to go to, our mothers called us in sick. My mother and I took a bag of preaudition sweet rolls over to the Woolfs' that morning, and while Jimmy and I split a jelly doughnut, we sat back and watched our mothers call the school and do a little acting of their own:

"This is Mrs. Hackett," my mother said. "Morgan won't be coming to school today; she's got a touch of the flu. Yes, *again*. I'm sure she'll be back on Monday. . . . Thank you." She hung up and handed the phone to Jimmy's mother. "You better be convincing, Enid—I think they're beginning to catch on. . . ."

"Do you realize, Fay," Mrs. Woolf said as she dialed, "that we're committing *perjury* for this young man? I wonder how many years we'll get for lying to an attendance office. . . ."

My mother smiled. "It'll be worth it when he's on Broadway."

"Hi, this is Mrs. Woolf," Jimmy's mother said. "Jimmy's not feeling well today; he won't be in school. . . . Oh, just the flu. He'll be back Monday. . . . 'Bye." When she hung up, she said, "They seem to think there's a lot of flu going around." She looked at my mother. "Must be an epidemic, wouldn't you say?"

My mother took a bite out of an almond sweet roll and nodded. "Absolutely," she said.

"Come on, Hackett," Jimmy said. "Let's get going or we'll miss our train."

"What's the hurry?" I asked. "We have twenty minutes—"

"We *could* have a flat tire, you know. Can we please get *going*?" He picked up his jacket and walked out of the kitchen.

I took a last sip of coffee. "Your son's impossible before he auditions for something, Mrs. Woolf."

"I know," she said. "You'll have to talk to him; knock some sense into him."

"I'll do my best."

"Come on, Hackett, will you?" Jimmy yelled.

I grabbed my sweater. "See you later. . . ."

When our train pulled out, it went past the tennis courts across the street from the school. My gym class was out chasing after lost balls and swinging their rackets in midair.

"Ha ha," I said. "It gives me such a good feeling to be going away from the school."

Jimmy was being uncharacteristically moody. He slumped in his seat and stared into space and didn't seem to hear a word I said.

"Did I tell you Mrs. Klein kept me after class last week?" I said. "She wanted to know why I didn't 'participate in class' more. Can you believe that? Wouldn't you think she'd appreciate having one quiet student in class?"

"You know something, Morgan," Jimmy said quietly, "you and I are too dependent on each other. We should try to make other friends at school—"

"We have friends," I said. "Well, maybe not close friends. But it's more important to have one good friend than it is to have a bunch of friends who don't mean anything—"

"We should try harder to fit in at school."

"Jimmy . . . what are you really trying to say?"

He looked at me and smiled. He held up his hands, and they were trembling. "I'm terrified."

"It's stage fright," I said. "You'll get over it. You always do."

"This is different. If I lose this, I'm losing much more than a part in a dinner-theater show—"

"Jimmy, you have to pretend you're in dance class

27

or something. Forget who you're dancing for. You'll make it. You're the best dancer I've ever seen."

"Do you know the kind of dancers I'm up against?"

"Do they know the kind of dancer *they're* up against?"

He smiled and shook his head and looked out the window.

There must have been a couple of hundred dancers lined up outside the entrance to the Shubert.

"God, *look* at that," I said.

Jimmy nodded. "See? What kind of chance do *I* have?"

"Jimmy, get going. Go *on*. What are you waiting for? An engraved invitation from the choreographer?"

"Thanks, Morgan. You're a real comfort. A source of inspiration."

"I try," I said.

Inside the theater, I had to catch my breath: The size of the place was enough to knock you over.

"Wow," I said.

"Maybe someday, Hackett, we'll *both* do a play here, huh?" He took off his jacket and tossed it to me. "Hang on to that, will you?"

"Hey, Jimmy," I said. "You better not mess up. . . ." He grinned and went down to the front of the theater with the other dancers. I slid onto an aisle seat in one of the back rows and waited for it all to start.

"Thank you all for coming!" the choreographer shouted. He stood in the middle of the stage with a clip-

28

board in one hand. "Please leave your résumés and eight-by-tens on the piano as you're called up onstage to dance. You will be dancing in groups of ten. The producers and I will then get together and decide if we want any of you to remain onstage and dance solo. Are there any questions? All right, then . . . let's get started."

It took a while for the actual auditioning to begin. First the clothes went flying. Jimmy and everybody else peeled down to tank tops and dance shorts, leotards and tights. During the warmup I understood why Jimmy had been so nervous: These dancers were probably the best in their schools, just like Jimmy was the best in his. I sat there and watched the auditioning start, and I wondered: How good do you have to be in order to beat out excellent?

Twenty minutes. Forty minutes. Group after group was called, with only a handful of dancers being asked to stay and dance solo. Finally it was Jimmy's turn. The choreographer shouted out staccato instructions: "STEP! KICK! TURN! STEP! KICK! KICK! Thank you!" And it was over. The choreographer and the producers got together in a huddle and talked. I held my breath. I crossed my fingers. Jimmy was trying to act very calm, but whenever he acts like he doesn't have a care in the world, I can be sure he's petrified. The choreographer walked over to the edge of the stage and looked at Jimmy. "You, step forward. The rest of you, thank you." I was jumping up and down inside. I watched Jimmy leap and twirl. Everything that was strength and grace seemed to be packed into those long legs of his. What a long way he had come from our porch-swinging days! When he finished, the choreographer thanked him with a noncommittal "Very nice. We'll call you."

I didn't wait for Jimmy to come back up the aisle. I flew down to the front of the theater and found him going through a pile of clothes, searching for his shirt and jeans.

"Not bad," I said. "Not bad at all."

He turned and looked at me. "What are you referring to? My audition or my legs?"

I threw his jacket at him. "What do *you* think?"

"Take it easy—even if I get the callback, that just means I made the finals. I'll still have another audition to pass."

"You drive me crazy the way you're so overcautious about everything!"

"I'm trying to be practical. I'm trying not to get my hopes up."

Sometimes nothing less than body contact will do. I threw my arms around his shoulders and whispered: "Just put your pants on, okay? Those legs of yours are driving all the girls in here and a few of the boys absolutely wild."

The jacket ended up on my head.

Jimmy's mother was out sweeping the front porch when we got home. When she saw us, she stopped the broom in mid sweep and leaned on it.

"How'd he do, Morgan?"

"He did great, Mrs. Woolf. They asked him to dance solo."

"They asked a lot of people to dance solo," Jimmy said. "It doesn't mean anything."

"Uh-huh," his mother said. She started sweeping the porch again. "Oh, Jimmy . . . by the way . . . someone called a few minutes ago and left a message for you."

"Who was it?"

"Someone from the city. Some . . . choreographer, I think. You're supposed to call him back—"

I don't think I've ever seen anyone move so fast. Mrs. Woolf's face broke into this terrific smile. She really has the neatest dimples I've ever seen.

"He got the callback," she said to me in a low voice, "but I wanted him to hear it from the choreographer."

"I knew he'd get it. You should have seen him. He was wonderful!"

"I think the biggest problem you and I'll have from now on is making sure he doesn't get too big for his britches."

"Not Jimmy," I said.

"I got it!" Jimmy yelled. He came flying out of the house and put his arms around his mother and whirled her around and around the porch. Then he grabbed me and did the same thing. "I got it, I got it, I got it!" he kept hollering.

"Jimmy, stop! I'm getting seasick!"

He stopped abruptly and I grabbed the porch railing. "What if I mess up?" he said. "What if I sprain an ankle or something?"

"Now, now, none of that talk," Mrs. Woolf said.

"When's your audition, Jimmy?"

"A week from tomorrow at four thirty."

"Want some company?"

"What do *you* think?" He put his arms around me and started to whirl me around again, but a bit more slowly this time. "You have to be there," he said. "You're my rabbit's foot. My four-leaf clover. And if I pass this audition, I'll buy you a steak dinner—"

"With onion rings?"

"Of course."

"And if you don't pass it?"

"Then you'll buy *me* one."

I didn't set eyes on Jimmy for five days. He stayed home from school and shut himself up in the dance studio in his basement and rehearsed for hours on end. Wednesday afternoon I called him up and he wouldn't even come to the phone.

"He's overrehearsing," Mrs. Woolf said. "I don't like to see him taking this audition quite so seriously. . . . Why don't you come over, Morgan? Maybe you can drag him out into the sunlight and talk some sense into him, huh?"

"You think he'll listen to *me?*"

"I think so. Come on over."

As soon as I pulled into Jimmy's driveway, I could hear music from the soundtrack of *Oklahoma!* blaring out of the basement windows. Mrs. Woolf came out to meet me, her hands over her ears.

"I've got the entire record memorized," she said. "I'm sure the whole neighborhood does too."

"You know what they say about geniuses, Mrs. Woolf. They're all obsessive about *something.*"

"Try to get him to take a break, will you? He's starting to lose his perspective, and I want him to be able to live with himself if he doesn't pass this audition. . . ."

"I'll talk to him."

I went in through the back of the house and opened the door to the basement. The music was deafening. I went down and sat on the stairs and watched him dance for a minute. He didn't even notice me. He was completely wrapped up in what he was doing: a quick series of spins, one after the other, around the perimeter of the studio. It made me dizzy watching.

"If you don't stop that, you're going to turn into butter," I said.

"Hi," he said. He went over and shut off the stereo, then leaned against the wall and tried to catch his breath. "What do you think?"

"I think you're sweaty."

"About the *dancing*."

"Oh. It looked good."

"I'm having trouble with the jetés."

"Your mother thinks you're taking this thing too seriously."

"Is that what she told you?"

"She says you're overrehearsing."

"God, Morgan . . . *you* understand how important this is, don't you?"

"Sure. I know. *Oklahoma!* You'll have to join Equity. You'll be on the road five months. Really the big time. I know."

"Try to contain your enthusiasm, will you?"

"So what happens when you overrehearse and pull a muscle, or you're so tired Saturday that you blow the audition? What happens then?"

He looked at me a minute. "My mother asked you to come over here and talk to me, didn't she?"

"What difference does it make?"

"It makes a lot of difference, Morgan." He got this wicked smile on his face. "She must think you have some sort of *power* over me."

"Well," I said, "don't I?"

"Maybe."

"So you'll take a break, then?"

"All right, Hackett, you win. I guess I've done enough dancing for today."

"Good. Let's forget about the audition, okay? Why don't we go downtown; get something to eat?"

34

"Is it all right if I take a shower first?"

"It's not only all right; I highly recommend it."

"Want to join me?"

"Maybe next time," I said.

Friday afternoon I was sitting in English struggling over a book report when Jody, this girl who sat next to me, gave me a nudge with her elbow.

"That cute guy you're always hanging around with," Jody whispered. "He's trying to get your attention. . . ." She nodded toward the door, and I saw Jimmy peeking around the doorjamb. He motioned for me to come out into the hall. Now, this was tricky. Getting out of Mrs. Klein's class for any reason was next to impossible. She didn't even issue a bathroom pass unless there was a puddle at your feet.

"What's going on?" Mrs. Klein asked. She looked at me, then out into the hall. Jimmy had disappeared.

"Nothing," I said.

"Are you okay now?" Jody said to me. She looked at Mrs. Klein. "Morgan felt faint a few minutes ago."

Mrs. Klein bit her lip and looked at me. She was trying to decide whether or not to believe what Jody had said. "Do you want to go to the nurse?"

I cleared my throat. "Uh, yeah . . ."

"I'll write a pass out for you."

I mouthed the words "thank you" to Jody, and she smiled and went back to her book. As soon as I had the pass, I went out into the hall and looked around.

Jimmy was standing in a small alcove next to the drinking fountain. He was carrying his duffel bag. His dance shoes were knotted and dangled from his shoulder.

"Do you know how much *trouble* you almost got me in?" I asked, waving the pass at him. "She only let me out of there because Jody told her I was sick. I'm supposed to be on my way to the nurse—"

"My audition's been moved up," he said. "I have to leave right now; do you still want to come?"

"Are you *crazy*? I can't just walk out of here!"

"What's the big deal? If your seventh-period teacher doesn't take roll, they'll never even miss you—"

"Yeah? And what if he does take roll?"

"Morgan, this isn't worth having a coronary over, okay? You don't have to come; I didn't want to leave without letting you know." He looked at his watch. "I've got to go; I'm driving in, and I don't know what traffic'll be like."

I stood there and watched him walk away. I balanced a couple of things in my head: one, going back to English and on to seventh period like I should, or two, going along with Jimmy and sitting in the back of that enormous theater and watching the outcome of his audition.

"Wait!" I whispered. I ran after him and caught up with him on the stairs, and damn him, he was *laughing*.

"I knew you'd come," he said.

"Don't be so cocky," I said. "And stop laughing.

36

Someday I might *not* come. Then maybe you wouldn't take me for granted."

We walked out of the building and down the hill to Crescent, where Jimmy's MG was parked. He threw his stuff into the back of the car, and we got in.

"I'm glad you're coming," he said.

"I don't know what happened, Jimmy. I just couldn't help myself."

He started the car. "Could it be, Morgan, that I have a certain power over *you*?"

"Maybe."

"How interesting."

I looked at him. "Shut up and drive."

4

I called my mother from a pay phone at the theater.

"Hi," I said. "Guess where I am."

"In the city at the Shubert," she said. "Enid called and told me about Jimmy's audition."

"I don't know when we'll be home. . . . It's almost four now, and they're just getting started—"

"You be careful, you hear? Don't go wandering around the city after it gets dark—"

"I'm not going to be *wandering* around—"

"Well," my mother said, "I never worry as long as I know Jimmy's with you."

"Sure. If any mugger tries to attack me, Jimmy'll just give him one quick tour jeté in the gut. Works every time. Better than a karate chop."

There was a sigh on the other end of the phone. "Honestly . . ."

"I've got to go see show business history being made," I said. "I'll call you in a little while; let you know how it went."

Jimmy was sitting down near the stage watching one of the other dancers audition. I tiptoed down the length of the theater, my steps in time to the music the pianist was playing. I slid into the seat behind Jimmy's and tapped him on the shoulder.

"I'm back," I said. "What did I miss?"

"The choreographer's been rejecting people right and left. . . . Christ, *look* at that guy up onstage, Morgan."

"What's wrong with him?"

"He's all technique and no style. . . . Dancing has to tell a story, especially in a play like this."

"Maybe he's nervous."

"Maybe he's a crappy dancer."

"Meow," I said.

"He *is*! *Look* at the guy, will you?"

"I'm looking at *you* right now, and I'm not too crazy about what I'm seeing."

"You wait till you're up against a hundred other actresses for a job, Morgan. Then we'll see how generous you are."

I didn't say anything. Jimmy was under a lot of pressure, so I decided I'd let him go on being a pain until the audition was over. After that he'd have to shape up.

"Thank you!" The choreographer shouted at the dancer onstage. "Next please!"

I watched the dancer walk down the wooden ramp

that led from the stage. "I guess you know a crummy dancer when you see one, Jimmy."

He turned in his seat to look at me. "Don't pay too much attention to the way I'm acting, Hackett. I get sort of crazy and hypercritical when I see the competition in action—"

"Don't you think I know you by now? You've been hanging around my life every day for seventeen years. . . ."

"If I make the play, you'll have a little breathing space. I'll be gone for five months."

"Yeah," I said. "I know."

But the truth is, I hadn't thought about his being gone until that moment. He had been a day-to-day part of my life for as far back as I could remember. It was going to feel very strange without him around.

"Cheer up," he said, looking at me over his shoulder. "Without me around to cramp your style, you'll probably have a torrid love affair with that hall monitor who's always drooling over you."

"Very funny. Just be careful who *you* drool over while you're on tour. Penicillin doesn't cure everything, you know."

"I'll keep it in mind. I'm going backstage to warm up, they have a barre set up there—"

"A bar, huh? Don't drink too much."

"Listen, Morgan—do me a favor, will you? Sit in the back of the theater while I audition, okay? I think . . . it'd be sort of hard to dance with you sitting right here near the front."

"I'll sit in the back row, all right? You won't even see me."

He grinned. "Thanks. See you later."

It didn't take me long to figure out the mechanics of the thing: The choreographer yelled, "Thank you!" at a dancer when he really meant "Take a hike!" I felt sorry for those rejected dancers. I couldn't imagine what it'd be like to finally get the chance to audition for an important show and then—bang!—have all your dreams yanked out from under you because you weren't the right type or maybe you were a little nervous or your tempo was a bit off.

I had to wait about a half hour for Jimmy to appear onstage. He walked slowly out to center stage, nodded to the pianist, and for about the ten millionth time that day I heard the first few notes of the *Oklahoma!* overture.

Jimmy started with a little something to grab their attention: a series of quick spins like he'd rehearsed in his studio, only something was different here.

Something was *wrong*.

I sat up straight in my seat. "Loosen up," I whispered. "Try to relax and be *yourself*! God, what are you *doing*?!"

These were not the free, confident moves of a professional dancer. Jimmy was moving around that stage

41

like a scared amateur. Even I could dance better than what he was doing up there, and brother, that is saying something.

"Thank you!" the choreographer shouted. The music stopped abruptly. So did Jimmy. He stood there like he'd been slapped across the face. "Next, please!" the choreographer yelled.

My heart sank. I watched Jimmy walk down the ramp. He stood by the stage and changed his shoes. He stuffed them into his duffel bag and started up the aisle. I didn't know what in the world I was going to say to him; I only knew I'd have to choose my words very, very carefully.

"Well," I said as he got closer, "look . . . there'll be plenty of other auditions—"

"Yeah, let's look on the bright side, Morgan. Let's just *do* that, huh?" He walked right past me and out of the theater.

"Jimmy, wait!" I ran and caught up with him out on the street, but he wouldn't stop to look at me, and he wouldn't slow down, either. I had a hard time keeping up with him. "Jimmy . . . look . . . I know how disappointed you are, but this isn't the end of the *world*—"

"Isn't it?"

"No! I don't understand why you're taking this so *hard*! You've lost other auditions before—"

"Did you *see* me up there? *Did* you?!"

"Yeah, I saw you! You got scared and it messed you up! So *what*? Next time it won't!"

"What are you, a dance expert? I've been dancing all my *life*!"

"And I've been watching you! You better get used to this, Jimmy, because the better the show, the tougher the competition. There are going to be a lot more rejections before you finally make it—"

"You're just real encouraging, Morgan, you know that? Real perceptive, too. How often do I *get* a chance like this? How soon do you think I'll get *another* one?"

"God, I cannot *believe* this is you! When are you going to start acting like a professional?"

"*Professional*?" He stopped and looked me right in the eye, a weird expression on his face. "What do you know about being a *professional*?"

"Careful, Jimmy . . ."

"You've never had the guts to go out for a real job, Morgan, and you don't know what it's like to lose one! You're just a lousy unprofessional!"

I felt I'd been socked in the stomach. I turned away from him before I started crying. I walked in the direction of the Shubert. I didn't know where I was going and I didn't particularly care.

"Come on, Morgan," Jimmy yelled. "Hey, come *on*! Don't be stupid! How do you think you're gonna get home?"

I didn't answer him. He was right, of course. I *was*

being stupid. I had no way of getting home to Glen Ellyn, not even enough money for a phone call, which meant I'd have to make the long trek over to my aunt's hospital and see if she'd float me a loan for train fare. I walked slowly for a while and tried to figure out why Jimmy'd acted the way he had. *What* he had said was bad enough, but the *anger* behind it all—that was something I couldn't understand and didn't know how to deal with.

I walked block after block, alternating feeling sorry for myself with being furious at Jimmy for leaving me alone to handle the fifty-seven varieties of weirdos that emerge in the city as darkness falls. My mother's words echoed in the back of my head: *I never worry as long as I know Jimmy's with you.*

Ha!

I wondered what she'd think of Saint Jimmy now.

5

I really felt like Jimmy had done one heck of a job beating me up from the inside out. He knew what he was doing, all right. He *wanted* to hurt me. That's what was starting to sink in. That's why I couldn't shake that socked-in-the-stomach feeling. When I got to the hospital, I took the elevator up to the psych floor and headed straight for my aunt's office. I couldn't wait to unload the story of my crummy afternoon on her. I knocked on the door to her office and stuck my head in, but it looked like she'd gone for the day. That's when I kicked the doorjamb. Hard.

"I broke my toes once, doing that," I heard my aunt say.

I turned around slowly. My aunt was leaning against the counter at the nurses' station. She was wearing a black linen suit and holding a bunched-up stethoscope in her hand.

"How long have you been standing there?" I asked.

"Long enough. You walked right past me."

"Oh."

"You don't look too good."

"I have a headache. Compliments of Jimmy Woolf."

"What happened?"

"I don't know. . . . Did you ever just have one of those days?"

"Sure," she said, smiling. She walked over and gave me a tug on my hair. "How do you think I broke my toes? Come on inside; tell me what's going on."

I followed her into the office. "I need to borrow some money. Jimmy left me stranded in the city without any way to get home."

"That doesn't sound like Jimmy," my aunt said. She sat down on the edge of her desk and took a pack of Tareytons out of her jacket pocket. "What happened exactly?"

"I don't *know!*" I slumped down into the chair in front of her desk. "I don't *know* what happened exactly! Jimmy blew his audition at the Shubert this afternoon and I was trying to . . . I just wanted to make him *feel* better! What's so terrible about *that?*"

"He took it out on you?"

"Are you *kidding?* He said some stuff to me—he *wanted* to make me feel bad! You should have seen the look on his face!" I could feel my eyes starting to fill up again. "Shit . . ."

"Okay," my aunt said quietly. "It's all right. Here." She pulled a couple of Kleenexes out of the box on her desk and handed them to me. I really felt like a jerk. "You and Jimmy will straighten things out—you always do."

"We had a pretty good thing going, and he screwed the whole thing *up*."

"Don't you think a friendship as good as yours and Jimmy's can withstand a little denting?"

"What I think," I said, "is that you should haul Jimmy Woolf in here and see if maybe there's another personality lurking around in his body, because he is definitely *not* himself."

My aunt lit her cigarette. She tilted her head slightly and looked at me. Whenever she looked at me that way, I was sure she could read my mind.

"Did you walk all the way over here from the Shubert?"

"Yeah."

She smiled. "Your mother would love that."

I blew my nose. "She doesn't have to know."

"How's your headache?"

"Compared to my day? Terrific."

"Tell you what—why don't you stay over with me so you don't have to make the trip home tonight, okay? I'll call Fay and tell her you're spending the night."

"That'd be nice. Thanks."

There was a knock on the door. Mrs. Getz, who was a nurse and a friend of my aunt's, poked her head in.

"Sorry to interrupt, but there's a call on line two—sounds kind of important."

"Who is it?" my aunt asked.

Mrs. Getz looked at me. "That friend of yours, Morgan—Jimmy, isn't it?"

"*Jimmy's* on the phone?" I said. "What does he want *now*?"

Mrs. Getz smiled. "He wants to talk to your aunt; that's all I know."

My aunt put out her cigarette. "Thanks, Betty."

Mrs. Getz left. My aunt reached for the phone.

"What are you *doing*?" I said. "You're not going to *talk* to him, are you?"

"You want me to hang up on him?"

"I don't know. Maybe."

"Why don't you go out to the nurses' station and ask Mrs. Getz to give you a couple aspirin for your headache, okay?"

"I'm staying right here. Go ahead and talk to him; I don't care. This might be interesting."

My aunt picked up the phone. "Jimmy? This is Dr. Hackett. . . . Yeah, I know. She came here. Uh-huh. . . . Let me put you on hold for a second, Jimmy; I'll see what I can do." She punched a button on the phone and looked at me. "He wants to talk to you."

"No! Why should I?"

"He sounds upset."

"*He's* upset!"

"Do you want to talk to him or not?"

"No! I don't know. I'm not sure. . . ."

My aunt picked up her stethoscope. "I'll meet you downstairs. I promised the E.R. doctors I'd stop by and take a look at one of their patients before I go home."

"Hey, what am I supposed to do about *Jimmy*?"

She thought a moment. "If you decide to talk to him, punch line two. Otherwise he'll be on hold for the rest of his life."

I sat and stared at the phone for a couple of seconds. Then I took a deep breath and picked it up. I punched line two.

"Jimmy?"

"Morgan . . . look . . . Christ, what'd you take off like that for?"

"You know why, Jimmy."

There was a pause. I could hear him breathing. I could hear traffic, like he was calling from a pay phone.

"Well, how are you going to get home? I'm just a few minutes away; I'll pick you up, okay?"

"I'm staying over at my aunt's tonight."

"Do you think she'd mind if I stopped by?"

"I'd mind, Jimmy."

"Look, I was *upset* earlier! Who wouldn't be? You know how much that audition meant to me!"

"That's a hell of an apology, Jimmy."

"God, what do you *want* from me?!"

"You try to figure it out," I said. "And when you do . . . call me."

I hung up quietly. I knew Jimmy had been trying

49

to tell me in a hundred different ways how sorry he was, but I wasn't ready to be friends again. Not yet. I guess I thought that making him feel bad would make *me* feel better, but all it did was make my head pound harder and leave me with an empty feeling that just wouldn't quit.

Getting even isn't all it's cracked up to be.

6

My aunt lives in a town house on the Near North Side of Chicago. When we got home, we parked in the garage and went in the back through the kitchen. Mrs. Rassin, my aunt's housekeeper, was standing at the butcher block chopping up vegetables for dinner.

"Well," she said. "Look who's here."

"Hi, Mrs. Rassin. What are you making?"

"Vegetable soup."

My aunt picked her mail up off the kitchen table and looked through it. "Morgan's going to stay over tonight. . . . She's had kind of a rough day."

"Oh, I'm sorry," Mrs. Rassin said. "Are you hungry? Some soup might taste good."

"Uh, I don't think I can eat anything, Mrs. Rassin. I just want to lie down for a while and see if I can get rid of this headache."

"You'd be surprised what a little soup can do. I'll bring a tray up to you."

My aunt looked at me and winked. "I'm going to take Morgan upstairs and get her settled."

"Oh, Dr. Hackett, the Danzigers called; they can't make your dinner party tomorrow."

"Hmm . . ." She picked up a piece of chopped carrot and popped it into her mouth. "I'll invite another couple. Maybe your folks would like to come," she said to me.

After we were on the stairs and safely out of Mrs. Rassin's earshot, I said: "You know how Mrs. Rassin is. In a minute she's going to bring up a bowl of soup and sit there to make sure I eat it, and Aunt Lo, I just can't eat anything right now."

She laughed. "I know. Mrs. Rassin thinks soup cures everything. What *do* you want?"

"A Coke?"

"I'll see what I can do."

My aunt has a very comfortable guest room. A guest room is supposed to be for guests in general, but I think I used it more than anyone else. A lot of my stuff from home was crammed into that room: stereo, records, books, tapes. I kicked off my shoes and flopped down onto the antique four-poster and stared at the ceiling. No problem making myself at home here.

"You're going to need something to sleep in tonight," my aunt said. She picked up the quilt folded at the foot of the bed and tucked it around me. "I'll get some pajamas out for you."

"How come they needed you down in the emergency

room this afternoon? Was it a suicide attempt or something?"

"Why?"

"I just think I'd feel better if I knew there was someone on the face of this planet who had a crummier day than I did."

"Someone did have a crummier day than you did. Jimmy."

"That jerk. I'm glad I hung up on him."

"I think you're mad at yourself for hanging up on him."

"He's a turkey, and I don't talk to turkeys!"

I could tell my aunt was trying not to laugh. She has this great warm laugh, and she laughs easily, too. "You know *why* Jimmy acted like such a turkey, don't you? He couldn't handle having you see him mess up."

I thought about that. I reversed the situation in my head: If I had messed up at an audition, who's the last person I'd want out there in the audience? Who's the last person I'd want walking beside me, trying to be understanding about the whole thing? Jimmy, of course.

"Dr. Hackett?" Mrs. Rassin hollered. "Your beeper's going off!"

"Damn," my aunt said. She sat down on the bed and grabbed the phone off the nightstand and dialed a number. "This is Dr. Hackett—what happened? . . . Okay. . . . All right, I'm on my way." She was on her feet in a tenth of a second. "Honey, I've got to go. Try to get some rest, okay? I'll leave something with Mrs. Rassin in case your headache gets worse."

After my aunt had gone, I thought a little about calling Jimmy and trying to patch things up, but then I decided it was too soon. I just wasn't sure what to say to him anyway. Then I started worrying about a bunch of crazy stuff: Like maybe what had happened between us was too big and maybe things wouldn't ever be set right again. I closed my eyes and tried to shut off the mental gymnastics, but my brain wouldn't settle down. I was sorry my aunt had had to go, because I wanted to talk some more and straighten out some things going on in my head.

But other people needed her too.

7

"I didn't think you'd ever wake up," Mrs. Rassin said when I opened my eyes. She walked over to the windows, opened the curtains, and the room suddenly filled with sun. I put my hands over my eyes.

"Gaa! What *time* is it?"

"Almost noon. Your aunt's been gone for hours. She said just to let you sleep."

"I didn't hear her come in last night."

"She didn't come home until midnight. It must have been a heck of an emergency, too; she really looked exhausted."

I threw the quilt off and sat up. My clothes looked like I'd bought them at a K Mart reduced table and then slept in them in a scrunched-up ball for about a hundred and fifty years.

"I don't suppose Jimmy called, did he?"

"No—was he supposed to?"

"I don't know. I guess not."

"Come on downstairs; I'll fix you something to eat."

"I can't eat anything when I first get up, Mrs. Rassin."

55

"You and your aunt! You know what *her* idea of breakfast is? A cup of coffee and a cigarette! I've been trying for years to get her to take better care of herself, but try to tell a doctor *anything*—"

"Okay, Mrs. Rassin, okay. I'll eat. Just for you."

We settled on a grilled cheese. I spent the rest of the afternoon watching Rocky-and-Bullwinkle reruns, cutting up cheese cubes for my aunt's party, thinking about Jimmy, and pondering the relative stupidity of the male-female relationship. It took me a good three or four hours to realize I was going to have to put my pride in my back pocket and make the first move. I brushed the cheese crumbs off my hands and picked up the phone. I had our conversation all planned. I was going to be really big about the whole thing while Jimmy fell all over himself trying to apologize, but it didn't quite work out that way.

His mother answered the phone:

"Hello?"

"Hi, Mrs. Woolf. Is Jimmy there?"

"No, he's out right now, Morgan; he's doing some shopping for me."

"How's he feeling? About the audition, I mean."

"Well, he's pretty philosophical about it—you know how he bounces back."

"He seemed kind of upset yesterday."

"Did he give you a bad time after the audition? He

mentioned something about your not driving home with him—"

"Well, I guess neither of us was in a very good mood. Would you ask him to call me? I'm at my aunt's."

"As soon as he gets back. It shouldn't be too much longer."

"Thanks, Mrs. Woolf."

My aunt came in about six. She was loaded down with her briefcase, medical bag, and two shopping bags from Saks.

"Now *this* looks intriguing," I said. "What did you get at Saks?"

She dumped everything beside me. "I got a few things for you so you'd have a change of clothes."

"You did? What? Can I see?"

"Mm-hmm . . ." She took a cigarette out of her coat pocket and lit it. "I talked to your mother last night—she and your father are coming to the dinner party tonight."

"Aunt Lo, I thought you weren't going to smoke anymore—"

"I'm tapering off. This is my last one."

"I've heard *that* before." I emptied the shopping bags. I started lifting lids and taking out tissue paper. She'd gotten me a short-sleeved angora sweater and a pair of wool slacks; also some sexy underwear that was all one piece.

"That's a teddy," my aunt said. "Your grandmother says she used to wear one when she was young—"

"I love it! Aunt Lo, you didn't have to do all this—"

"I *wanted* to." She sank down onto the couch. I watched the stream of smoke from her cigarette, and I looked at her. Mrs. Rassin had been right: She really did look exhausted.

"How was your emergency last night?" I asked. "Mrs. Rassin said you didn't get in till late."

"It's all under control." She never specifically mentioned any of her patients. I knew she was a good psychiatrist, partly because she was a good listener, but mostly because of her common sense. You could talk and talk and talk to her and she could cut right through to what you were trying to say, or trying *not* to say. I thought maybe she had picked up this talent in medical school, but my father said she had always been that way, even as a little kid.

"Is your sweetie going to be here tonight?" I asked. "The famous Dr. Petrie?"

A slow smile crept over my aunt's face. "Mm-hmm."

"What was it like?" I said. "You know . . . when you first knew you were in love with him?"

"It was very romantic," my aunt said. "We'd been talking about the upcoming flu season, as I recall, and he looked deeply into my eyes and said: '*Loey—let's inoculate each other.*' "

"What really happened?"

"Well," she said, leaning forward to tap her cigarette against the inside of the ashtray, "I haven't gotten the flu yet, have I?"

I gathered up my new clothes and stuffed them back into the shopping bags. "I think I'll go upstairs. This conversation is definitely getting X-rated."

I went up to the bathroom and peeled off my wrinkled clothes and took a quick shower. I was really in the mood for a good party. I just wanted to be around people who were laughing and talking and having fun, as opposed to one slightly demented seventeen-year-old dancer who'd obviously forgotten how to put his finger in the phone and dial. I grabbed a big, thick towel and took my time drying off, then I stepped into the teddy my aunt had gotten me. It was white and silky and had lacy cutouts on it. Wearing it made me feel like a very sexy person, which is a feeling you don't get when you wear cotton underpants with little pink flowers all over them. I looked at myself in the mirror and wondered if anyone of any import would ever see me wearing this. So far the only people who had ever seen me in my underwear were the other girls in my gym class, and half of them didn't even *believe* in underwear. I adjusted the straps, and when I turned around and looked over my shoulder to see how I looked from another angle, I heard a familiar voice.

"It looks as nice from the front as it did from the back."

I whipped my head around and saw Jimmy standing there.

"Jesus!" I said.

Jimmy looked around. "Is He here too?"

8

"What are you *doing* here?" I yelled.

"Enjoying the view."

"God!"

"You've got to stop name-dropping like that, Morgan."

"Jimmy, do you *mind*?" I grabbed my new sweater and held it in front of me.

"Oh, come on. I've seen you with a lot less on. Remember the time we took a bath together?"

"Hardly," I said. "And neither do you. We weren't even three at the time."

"Some things you don't forget. Not if they're memorable enough." He wandered into the room and stretched out on the bed. "Well, are you going to stand there half naked, or are you going to get dressed?"

I frowned at him and pulled my sweater on. "What are you *doing* here?"

"Your aunt invited my parents and me to dinner."

"She *what*?"

"Didn't she tell you?"

"No, she did *not*! If I had *known* that . . . if I'd had even the slightest inkling you'd be coming, do you think there's even the remotest possibility I'd be *standing* here now?"

"It's a little hard to take that speech seriously, Morgan, when you're standing there without any pants on." He picked up my slacks and threw them to me.

"You acted like a real bastard yesterday, Jimmy."

"God, your *language*—"

"You think I'm kidding?" I pulled my pants on and zipped them up. "You think I can just *forget* some of the stuff you said to me?"

"Morgan . . . look . . . you know I didn't mean any of that stuff—"

"You meant it."

"You know what it's like to make a total jackass out of yourself and know your best friend's out in the audience *watching*?!"

"You didn't make a jackass out of yourself until *after* the audition, Jimmy."

"All right, Morgan, okay . . . if that's the way you want it . . ." He stood up and grabbed one of the pillows off my bed. "Why don't we settle this thing physically, huh?"

"*Physically!*"

"A pillow fight."

"You're crazy!"

He started swinging at me. "When we were kids, a good pillow fight always got you out of a bad mood."

"Well, we're not kids now and I'm not going to fight you."

"Arm yourself, Hackett—"

"No! This is silly!"

"Defend yourself!"

"Quit swinging that pillow at me, dammit! You almost hit me in the face!"

"I'm not aiming for your face, Hackett." He swung at me again, and this time, well, let's just say that this time he caught me south of the border.

"You're really asking for it, Jimmy."

"Tell me about it."

"I refuse to lower myself to your level."

"That's right, Morgan. Let's be mature about this." He hit me across the shoulders.

"Jimmy Woolf, you do that once more and I'll—" The pillow came down on my head.

"All right! You want war?! You've got it!" I grabbed the other pillow off my bed and hit him in the stomach. He countered by letting me have it across the back. After a few minutes of vigorous warfare I was helpless, completely out of breath. I collapsed on the bed. So did Jimmy.

"Okay," I said. "Okay. You win."

"Morgan . . . listen . . . I still can't believe I acted like such a jerk yesterday. God, you're the last person in the world I'd want to hurt."

I stared at the ceiling. "I know. It's okay. All is forgiven."

"You sure?"

"Sometimes I think . . . sometimes I worry that, you know, the older we get, the more we pull away from each other."

"We're not pulling away from each other."

"Aren't we? Our lives are already starting to go in different directions. It's just going to be hard for me, that's all, when you *do* go on tour with a play and aren't around anymore. . . ."

He leaned on his elbow and looked at me. "Morgan, are you going to cry?"

"No," I said.

"Yes, you are—you're going to cry."

"I am not."

"Did anyone ever tell you you have a sense of the dramatic?"

"Only you," I said.

"It'll come in handy when you get your first big break."

I grabbed my pillow and gave him a final whack.

"Looks like things are back to normal," my aunt said. She was standing in the doorway putting on her earrings. She looked beautiful: Her hair was pulled back with a silver barrette, the earrings were diamonds, as was her bracelet, and she wore a tailored silk blouse and a long skirt. I could smell her perfume from the bed.

"Wow," I said.

"I look okay, then?"

"I'll say. Where'd you get those diamonds?"

"I'll tell you when you're older. Why don't you both come downstairs. Dinner won't be too long."

Jimmy jumped off the bed and grabbed my hands and pulled me to my feet. "Come on, Hackett. Let's party."

"Do you mind if I finish getting ready?"

"Go ahead." He started out the door. "Don't listen to a thing she says, Dr. Hackett. *She* attacked *me*! She had me pinned to the bed, and for a second there I didn't know *what* she had in mind—"

"Jimmy, just go cram a few thousand Ritz crackers into your mouth so you can't talk, okay?"

"Okay. See you in a minute."

After he was gone, I said to my aunt, "How come you didn't tell me he was coming?"

"It was a last-minute thing," my aunt said. "It must have slipped my mind."

"Uh-huh. Well, anyway . . . I guess you were right. About Jimmy and me, I mean. . . . I guess our friendship's stronger than I thought."

"You and Jimmy really have something special going for you."

"Yeah," I said. "And it only took me seventeen years to realize it."

9

"Well, now . . . Dr. and Miss Hackett," my father said when my aunt and I came downstairs. He took my aunt's hands and twirled her around. "Pretty dressed up, Loey—anyone special coming tonight?"

"Maybe," my aunt said.

"Morgan tells us you're going with someone from the hospital. When do we get to meet him?"

"He'll be here tonight."

"Oh?" My father looked at me and winked. "Maybe I should ask him if his intentions are honorable."

"I can save you the trouble," my aunt said. "They're *not*."

"Sounds like I better have a little talk with this guy—"

"You do," my aunt said, pulling him close, "and I will cheerfully plant an axe between your ears."

My father and my aunt always sound like they're playing war games, but they're really very close. And when my aunt's date did arrive, my father was the one who greeted him and introduced him to my mother and Mr. and Mrs. Woolf. Jimmy went up to him and shook his hand right away, but I went over to the bar and took more time than I needed pouring myself a Coke. It's just really hard for me to meet new people, but I noticed that Dr. Petrie seemed a little shy, too. I couldn't picture him specializing in emergency medicine and buzzing around the hospital the way he probably did.

I took my Coke and went over to the couch, where my mother and Mrs. Woolf were sitting.

"What do you think of him?" I asked. I sat on the edge of the coffee table and helped myself to a handful of Cheese Puffs.

"He's very attractive," my mother said. "How serious *is* it? Has she said anything to you?"

"Well, they gave each other flu shots, if that means anything."

"Your mother's already planning the wedding," Mrs. Woolf said. "You get to be maid of honor and I get to be in charge of the bridal shower."

My mother took another look at Dr. Petrie. "They'd have great-looking kids together."

"God, Mother!"

"What?"

"Don't you think you're rushing things a bit?"

"Face it, Morgan," Mrs. Woolf said. "Your mother's an incurable romantic. You should have heard her the

67

week you and Jimmy were born. We were still in the maternity wing at the hospital, and she was all set to arrange a marriage between you two—"

"Jimmy and me? No. Absolutely not. There is no way we'd ever—"

"Okay, so I'm a romantic," my mother said. "I like the idea of two people being meant for each other, the idea that you and Jimmy would grow up together and maybe someday . . . well, anyway, the two of you looked so cute, lying right next to each other in the hospital nursery—"

"*Please!*" I turned to Mrs. Woolf. "I love Jimmy, but Mrs. Woolf, your son is way too flaky to marry—"

"That's funny," my mother said. "Jimmy says the same thing about *you.*"

"Never mind," I said. "Let's not change the subject here. I just think you should let Aunt Lo live her own life and not pressure her to get married or anything."

"Who's pressuring her? I'd just like to see her start thinking seriously about marriage, that's all."

"I think she wants to try it out before she makes any permanent plans."

"Try it out—what does *that* mean?"

Mrs. Woolf laughed and put her hand on my mother's. "I hate to break this to you, Fay, but I think Morgan's trying to tell you that your sister-in-law and Dr. Petrie are having some sort of torrid assignation."

My mother just looked at me. "You mean they're *sleeping* together?"

I choked a little on my Coke. "Mother, no one says 'sleeping together' anymore."

"No? What *do* they say?"

"Aunt Lo and Dr. Petrie are co-vivants . . . on a part-time basis, that is—"

"Co-vivant—what does *that* mean?"

"It's French," I said. "For sleeping together."

"How charming," my mother said.

After dinner, after everyone had left the table and wandered into the living room, Jimmy and I took our coffee and headed for our favorite spot: a window seat at the front of the house. I sat sideways and stretched my legs out on Jimmy's lap.

"Why don't you make yourself comfortable, Hackett. Hey, watch it! You're making me spill my coffee!"

"You have bony knees, Jimmy."

"No one else has complained."

"I thought *I* was the only girl who'd experienced your knees firsthand!"

"You have an interesting way of putting things, Morgan. Listen—there's something I want to talk to you about. Since I'm obviously not ready for the big time, I've decided to go back to Pheasant Run and do their children's theater again—"

"Are you *kidding*? Last year you said you were through with children's theater forever. Remember the time that kid bit you on the ankle and you had to have stitches?"

"Yeah, they should have given me a rabies shot while they were at it."

"I remember your exact words. You sat on the edge of the stage clutching your ankle, and you said: 'Nobody's *this* desperate for work. Never again.' "

"Well, that was before my rather spectacular flop at the Shubert. Anyway, I was telling the director at Pheasant Run about you—"

I looked at him. "About me? Why'd you think he'd be interested in *me*? I'm just a . . . what was the phrase you used? Oh, yeah—I'm just a *lousy unprofessional*, remember?"

"Look . . . I just . . . I feel really bad I said that, and this is my own inadequate little way of making up for it, okay? There's an opening for an apprentice out at Pheasant Run, and I thought you might be interested in it—"

"An apprentice? Me?"

"Sure. Why not? It'd be fun for us to work together, wouldn't it?"

I took a sip of coffee. "Is this a bribe, Jimmy?"

"Yes, Morgan, this is a bribe. You know I'd do anything to see that smile of yours—"

"Let me get something straight before I flash anything at you that even remotely resembles a smile. You think I'd be willing to work hours on end for no pay? To skip my acting workshops at Second City just so I can hang around Pheasant Run and be an apprentice for a *kids'* show? You think I'd be interested in that?"

"Well," he said, "No one could ever call you a *lousy unprofessional* again. . . ."

I pictured myself on the very lowest rung of the show-business ladder with a long climb ahead of me, but that was okay. As long as Jimmy was on the same ladder I was, the length of the climb didn't seem too important.

"How about it, Hackett?" Jimmy said. "You interested in being Pheasant Run's resident slave?"

"Maybe."

"Well? Where's my smile?"

"You really are a turkey, Jimmy," I said, smiling at him. "It's right here. Right where it's always been."

∽ 10 ∼

I started my apprenticeship on a cold rainy Thursday in early November. Jimmy drove me out to Pheasant Run and gave me the official tour about five minutes before rehearsal started.

"Now, Miss Hackett," he said, pulling me onstage, "directly in front of you is your audience area. Please keep your eyes on your ankles at all times and beware of children with extremely sharp teeth."

"I'll watch out, professor. Anything else?"

"I take my coffee black."

"Really? You may find yourself wearing it instead of drinking it."

In the next five minutes a whole bunch of people came in. I got to meet the director, this young bearded guy named Ben Kubelsky. He handed me an empty coffeepot and a stack of scripts.

"Welcome to the glamorous world of the theater, Morgan. Jimmy'll show you where we keep the coffee, and would you pass out those scripts? Thanks a lot; it's great having you with us."

I turned to Jimmy. "He's kidding, right? I'm not really supposed to make the *coffee*, am I?"

"Yeah, Morgan. In between the time you walked in that door and the time you collect your Oscar, you're gonna have to do all those crummy little jobs no one else wants to do."

"Jimmy . . . I don't *do* coffee."

"Morgan, once upon a time I did coffee, Ben did coffee, and now you're gonna do coffee." He went over to the sink and found a can of Chase & Sanborn. He balanced it on my stack of scripts. "Look at the bright side," he said. "After Ben *tastes* your coffee, you probably won't have to make it anymore."

"I'll do it," I said. "But I don't have to *like* doing it."

Jimmy hit me on the arm. "That's the stuff, Hackett. You're a real trouper."

I made the coffee. I poured it into Styrofoam cups, delivered it to the actors, ran for cream and sugar. I felt like a damn waitress. The closest I came to doing anything "theatrical" was handing out the scripts—Dickens' A *Christmas Carol*. I saved the last script for Jimmy. I delivered it airmail across the stage. It hit him in the stomach.

"*This* is supposed to be the beginning of my great theatrical career?"

"All right, Morgan. Okay."

"Did you see that *jerk* over there send me down to the gift shop for Rolaids? Why should *I* be responsible for *his* heartburn?"

"Morgan, come on; you don't have to be so dramatic—"

"Yes, I do! This is a *theater* and I *want* to be dramatic!"

"You know what you do when you pout? You stick your lower lip out like this—"

"I'm not pouting."

"You want to run lines with me until Robin gets here?"

"Who's Robin?"

"My girlfriend . . . *Scrooge's* girlfriend. She's in the scene where the Ghost of Christmas Past shows Scrooge all the stuff he missed out on by being so cheap—"

"Yeah, I know the story, Jimmy." I took the script from him and leafed through it. "What's she like?"

"Scrooge's girlfriend?"

"No. Robin."

"Why?"

"Just curious."

"What difference does it make? She's a girl, that's all. Will you please just cue me on my lines?"

While I was doing the scene with Jimmy, I noticed Ben standing off to the side watching us. I thought about how neat it'd be if he came over and said something like: "Robin can't make it, but it looks like you can handle the part. How about it?" Only what happened instead was Ben came over to tell me they needed more coffee, and while I was making it this long-legged

74

ballerina-type girl walked up to Jimmy and gave him a pretty serious kiss. I was so shocked I knocked the Mister Coffee over.

"Hey, Morgan!" Jimmy yelled. "Robin's here; I need my script!"

"All right! Okay! Just a minute!" I grabbed some paper towels and soaked up the coffee. Watching Jimmy laugh like a lunatic with Robin over there really gave me a creepy feeling. I wiped his script off and took it over to him, but I felt like I was butting in on a big private meeting.

"Is there anything *else*?" I said.

"No. . . . Oh, Morgan, I want you to meet Robin."

Robin and I smiled at each other.

"Morgan's working as an apprentice for the run of the play," Jimmy said.

"Don't worry; it'll get better," Robin said. "Ben usually tries to give the apprentices a chance to do some acting before the play closes."

"Uh-huh," I said.

Jimmy tried opening his script, but the pages were all stuck together. "You got coffee all *over* this!"

"Don't worry," I said. "It's decaffeinated."

I sat off to the side and watched Jimmy and Robin rehearse. I almost walked out, I really did. I hadn't spent over a year and a half in an acting workshop just so I could run around getting coffee for everyone and watch Jimmy drool over some Junior Miss reject who was built like a tongue depressor. By the time rehearsal was over, I was fed up with being an apprentice, fed up with the theater in general, and fed up with Jimmy in particular.

On the way home I told him so.

"I think maybe it was a mistake. This apprentice thing, I mean. I'm not sure I'm cut out for the glamorous world of the theater."

"Come on, Hackett . . . you won't *always* be running around on Mickey Mouse errands. Sooner or later you'll get a chance to act—"

"How long have you known Robin?"

"Robin?"

"Yeah. Robin. The girl who had her lips planted all over you. How long have you known her?"

"We've done some plays together; she's an old friend—"

"*We're* old friends too, but I don't go around *kissing* you all the time—"

"No one's stopping you from kissing me, Morgan—"

"*I* could play Scrooge's girlfriend just as good as that toothpick you were mauling. Better, probably."

"What have you got against Robin?"

"She's just a *face*, Jimmy, that's all. She can't act. . . . What's so *funny*?"

"Are you listening to yourself?"

"She can't act! I'm serious! And I don't think it was

76

too professional of her to sneak up behind you like that and cop a feel!"

"You're talking like a jealous woman, Hackett."

"Jealous!"

"You can only keep your hormones on a leash for just so long, Morgan. Then sooner or later—"

"You're crazy!"

"Face it, Hackett, some other female has invaded your territory and you're insanely jealous."

"You have an absolute faculty for—"

"I wish you could have seen the look on your face—"

"You have an absolute *genius* for—"

"—when Robin was kissing me."

"—misinterpreting everything I SAY!"

"I guess it's only normal for you to feel a little possessive—"

"Don't make me laugh!"

"Why not? It's pretty funny, isn't it?" He glanced over at me. "*Isn't* it?"

"Yeah! Very!" I looked away from him. "Okay, maybe it's true. Maybe I've had you to myself for so long, I'm just not willing to share you with anyone."

"You're not really serious about quitting the apprentice thing, are you?"

"No . . . I guess not. . . ."

"You don't have anything to worry about, Morgan."

"I don't?"

77

"No—Robin's nothing compared to you."

I didn't say anything else on the way home. Neither did Jimmy. He turned on the radio and we listened to some rock on WLS. I felt pretty good. That was something I could never figure out about Jimmy: Somehow he always said what I needed to hear.

~ 11 ~

My big chance to do some acting came a couple of weeks before Christmas. I was lugging a pile of costumes up to the dressing rooms when Ben stopped me on the stairs.

"You have Robin's costume in there?"

"Yeah, I think so. It just came back from the cleaners."

"Think you could fit into it?"

"Excuse me?"

"Robin's cramming for her midterms tonight. You want to go on for her?"

"Go on for her. . . ."

"You've got an hour before curtain; you can get up in the part by then, can't you? There's not that much to memorize."

"I'm not—Robin doesn't have an understudy?"

Ben smiled. "Morgan, I guess you've realized we're not the Shubert or the Blackstone or any of those. When we need an understudy, we grab anyone we think'll fit into the costume. How about it?"

"Yeah, I'd like to, but . . . Robin's a lot thinner than I am. I'm not sure her dress'll fit—"

"It'll fit better on you than it will on Jimmy. Go try it on, okay? I'll get you a script and we'll run through your scene."

"Okay. Thanks."

I took the stairs two at a time. I ran down the hall and pounded on the men's dressing-room door.

"Hey, Jimmy!" I yelled. "You decent?!"

"You should know better than to hand me a straight line like that, Morgan!"

"I've got your costume here!"

The door opened. He was standing there in his underwear.

I tossed him his costume. "Here," I said. "Put some clothes on."

"I think I left my black shoes in the car. I don't suppose you'd—"

"Forget it. I'm through being a slave, Jimmy. I've been promoted." I turned around and headed for my dressing room. Jimmy tried walking beside me and pulling on his pants at the same time.

"Promoted to what?" he said.

"Robin's not here today, so I'm going on for her."

"Really?"

"Yeah, really. I'm your new co-star. Surprised?"

"No, I'm just trying to figure out how you did it."

"Did what?"

80

"Got rid of Robin—what'd you do? Slip her some poison? Shove her down the stairs? What'd you do?"

"Don't be a jerk! She's studying for midterms or something." I walked into the dressing room and hung the costumes on the wardrobe rack. "Would you please turn around? I've got to get dressed—"

"You want me to turn around? After all we've been through together?"

"Turn AROUND!"

He shrugged and turned around. I pulled off my sweatshirt and wriggled out of my jeans.

"You know something, Morgan—a lot of famous people have started this way. The star breaks a leg, the understudy goes on, and as fate would have it, there just happens to be a talent scout from MGM in the audience—"

"You're *laughing* at me!"

"I am not!"

"You think this is funny!"

"I do not!"

I pulled Robin's dress over my head. "Let me tell you something, Jimmy. You've done a million plays out here, so this isn't a big deal to you. But this is my *first* play here, and it's a big deal to me. Understand?"

"Yeah, I understand."

"Good. Zip me up."

81

He turned around and started tugging at the dress. "This is gonna be a tight squeeze, Morgan—"

"God, your hands are cold!"

"Yeah, that's what Robin always says—"

"Very funny! Gaa!" The dress zipped. I could hardly breathe.

"Not bad, Hackett—you fill it out a lot better than Robin does. Robin doesn't have . . . Robin's not as . . . she's a little less—"

"I know there's a compliment in there somewhere, Jimmy. I accept it, okay? Just tell me what I need to know to get through this play."

"You've been watching Robin do it, haven't you? You have—what—about ten lines in the second act, that's all. Don't worry, I'll help you out if you get stuck."

"Morgan!" Ben hollered. "You ready? Come on down; we'll do a quick run-through!"

"This is *it*, Morgan," Jimmy whispered. "A star is born!"

"Good grief," I said.

Ben nodded at me when Jimmy and I walked out onstage. There's just something kind of neat and romantic about walking out onto a bare stage, when there isn't any proper lighting to cover up all the marks and scratches.

Ben handed me a script. "We'll have a bench set

up for you downstage during the play, but for now let's just run through the scene, okay?"

I flipped through the script. It was sort of nerve-racking, jumping into the middle of the play like that and knowing that even if I *was* lousy, they were stuck with me because the dress fit.

> ME (*playing Belle, about to kiss off young Scrooge*): It matters little! It matters little to you that another idol has taken my place!
>
> JIMMY (*playing Scrooge*): What idol, Belle?
>
> ME In these last six years a golden one!
>
> JIMMY I am not changed toward you, am I?
>
> ME When our contract was made, you were another man—
>
> JIMMY I was a boy!
>
> ME Your own feeling tells you that you were not what you are . . . .

I was actually doing some *real* acting! Okay, maybe it was just a kids' show and maybe it *wasn't* exactly an award-winning performance, but I was rehearsing for a real play, not just doing an exercise in an acting workshop that some audience would never see. I felt like I did the first time I rode my bike without training wheels: scared, excited, all of that.

"Not bad," Ben said when I finished. "One thing, though, Morgan; remember, we've got an audience full of kids here, so you're gonna have to be loud enough to drown out their talking."

"Kids make an interesting audience," Jimmy said. "Once when I was doing a play here, I had a kid walk across the stage, tug on my pants, and ask me to take him to the bathroom."

"What'd you do?"

"What *could* I do? I took him."

"In the middle of the play?"

"Well, I thought about *not* taking him, but then I considered the consequences. . . ."

"That kid took a curtain call with you, didn't he?" Ben asked.

Jimmy nodded.

I'm lucky. I'm a pretty quick study. I learned my lines while the lady who played the Ghost of Christmas Past pulled my hair back into a semidecent Victorian hairdo. She lent me her makeup kit, and I attacked my face the way I'd seen Robin do hers: lots of pancake, blush, dark eyeliner, too, so they could see my eyes way in the back of the theater. I'd just finished when Jimmy stuck his head into the dressing room.

"Well, it's now or never, Hackett. You ready?"

"I guess," I said. "Yeah, I'm ready."

*   *   *

It was pitch-black backstage except for a little light over the clipboard the stage manager was holding. He motioned for us to take our places behind the curtain. Standing backstage and waiting to go on has to be one of the great highs of all time. It's probably a mixture of nerves, anticipation, excitement, and adrenaline all rolled into one.

"Hey," I whispered to Jimmy. "I think I'm getting nervous."

"You don't have *time* to get nervous." He took my hand. "You can get nervous later. I'll remind you, okay?"

"You're always so practical, Jimmy."

"One of us has to be."

Out onstage Old Scrooge was ranting and raving at the Ghost of Christmas Past. This was a pretty watered-down version of the Dickens' classic, but even so I could hear some of the kids fidgeting or talking, shuffling their feet. I knew if I could hold my own in front of *them*, I could probably handle *any* audience.

The Ghost of Christmas Past gave our cue: "My time grows short! Quick!"

The stage manager threw a switch and the lights onstage came up. Jimmy and I ducked around the curtain, stepped onstage. I couldn't see beyond the footlights, but I *felt* all the people out there. I took a deep breath, started across the stage, caught my toe on something, and fell forward. Flat on my face. I got the wind knocked out of me but good. It seemed like I was on that floor for a hundred years, although I know it was only a second or two before Jimmy was beside me, helping me up.

"Look at me," he whispered. "*Look* at me. Come on; you're okay." It was hard for me to take my eyes off the actor and actress playing Scrooge and the Ghost of Christmas Past. They looked as shocked as I felt.

I looked at Jimmy, locked my eyes into his, let him lead me to the bench set up downstage. All the lines I'd memorized had been knocked clear out of my head. I couldn't even talk; I was too numb.

"Belle, how many times have I told you," Jimmy said, "stay away from that rum punch; you know what a kick it has."

The audience roared. Some of them applauded. I was vaguely aware that Jimmy had done something good, that he had pulled the audience over to our side. I sat there, paralyzed, while Jimmy rewrote our Dickens dialogue into a minimonologue. It started like this:

JIMMY   I know you think a golden idol has re-
placed you in these last six years,
Belle . . . .

Slowly, things started coming into focus. The pain started to register where I'd whacked my left knee, and the whole humiliation angle began to sink in. It takes a while for things to hit me, but when they hit, they hit hard. I sat there watching Jimmy bail me out, and I knew I was going to cry. I was going to cry a *lot*, and I couldn't wait to get off that damn stage.

12

I think I got off the stage without anyone seeing me fall completely apart. I brushed past Ben backstage. He said something like: "Look, try not to be too upset," but I didn't stick around to hear anything else. I pushed open the stage door and clanked down the metal steps to the parking lot. I leaned back against the building and watched the traffic on North Avenue, watched the snow flurries float past the parking-lot lights. I don't know what the hell I thought I was doing, crying all alone in a parking lot at night. I really do dumb stuff when I'm rattled.

"Christ—what are you doing out *here*?"

I looked up. Jimmy was just starting down the stairs.

"Jimmy, just leave me alone for a few minutes, okay?"

"You don't look too good, Morgan."

"I'm okay."

"You always do that. You always say you're okay even when it's perfectly clear you're not okay at all."

"I said I'm OKAY!"

"All right, Morgan. Be tough. Have it your own way. . . ." I just stood there, biting my lip and staring at the parking lot. I was barely hanging on. Jimmy walked around in front of me and took off his coat. He wrapped it around me and pulled me close. I rested my cheek on his chest, and I felt like everything was breaking down inside me: I really started crying hard.

"I'm never going out on a stage again!"

"Sure you are."

"I'm supposed to be an actress! I'm supposed to be an actress, and I can't even walk across a *stage*!"

"Morgan . . . you know how many people screw up the first time they go on? It's practically a theatrical tradition—"

"Ben'll never let me go on for Robin or anyone else again—"

"Yes he will."

"I'll be lucky if he even lets me go back to making the *coffee*!"

"Morgan . . ."

"I'm not kidding! God, I cannot *believe* I walked out in front of hundreds of people and fell flat on my face!"

"Morgan?"

"What?"

He hugged me tight. "Shut up."

I shut up.

"Now, listen. You remember a conversation we had a while back in front of the Shubert Theater? Huh? You remember that?"

"Yeah . . ."

"Yeah? You remember how crummy I did at that audition? You remember how I screwed up?"

"Yeah. I remember."

"*Everyone* screws up, Hackett. It's a big club."

"I'm never going out there again, Jimmy."

"You have to take your curtain call."

"Are you *crazy*?" I pulled his handkerchief out of his vest pocket and blew my nose. "Take a curtain call? They'd laugh me off the stage!"

"No one's going to laugh at you."

I took off his coat and tossed it to him. "No one's going to *laugh* at me because I'm not going out there. Not after what happened."

"You've got to. Especially after what happened."

"I don't believe in all that 'the show must go on' crap, Jimmy."

"If you don't go back out on that stage now, you never will."

"Fine."

He took my hand. "And I'd hate to see that happen, Morgan, because I *know* how badly you want to act."

I frowned at him. "Jimmy, let *go* of me."

"After the play, Morgan."

I tried pulling my hand away, but he held on tight. "Jimmy, this isn't *funny*! Let go of me, DAMMIT!"

"Later."

"You're crazy! I won't go with you!"

"No?" He started pulling me up the stairs. It was no fair: As kids we had been evenly matched, but somehow he ended up stronger.

"Jimmy, I just want you to know that as of now you can consider our friendship permanently *canceled*!"

"Yeah, yeah, yeah . . ."

"You think I'm *kidding*?"

"No, Morgan, I don't think you're kidding. . . ." He opened the stage door and pulled me inside. He didn't let go of me, either. When I saw Ben walking over to us, I was all set to fly out the door again, only this time I couldn't.

"You okay?" Ben said. "You didn't hurt yourself when you fell, did you?"

I cleared my throat. "No. I'm okay. Thanks."

"Well. It'll go better next time. You'll see."

I heard the audience applauding, so I knew the play had ended. Most of the actors who'd been hanging around backstage started lining up two by two for the curtain call. Jimmy very casually walked me over there. Anyone who didn't know better would have thought we were such good friends we just naturally wanted to hold hands.

"I'll never *forgive* you for this, Jimmy!"

"You're getting yourself all upset for nothing, Morgan."

"I mean it! *Never!*"

The couple in front of us stepped around the curtain and onto the stage.

"Ben likes us to do a little bow when we take the curtain call," Jimmy whispered.

"Forget it! I'm not bowing! I'm not doing *anything*!"

Jimmy shrugged. "Do whatever you want." He walked around the curtain and pulled me with him. I honestly thought I was going to pass out—that's how scared I was. I don't know what I expected: a hostile audience with a bushel of tomatoes, maybe. The stage lights were up. Jimmy and I walked to center stage; then that *jerk* let go of me. He turned to the audience, bowed, and exited stage right. I stood there all alone on that stage like an idiot. I took a quick bow. The audience kept on applauding, and no one hurled any vegetables at me. I actually got off the stage without being laughed at, without falling on my face, without *anything* happening. Backstage, no one came up to tell me I'd ruined the play. They were all too busy, undressing on the way upstairs, talking and laughing.

I changed out of Robin's dress and back into my sweatshirt and jeans. I washed my face and combed out what was left of my Victorian ringlets. There was a knock on the door.

"Who is it?" I said.

"Your former friend."

"Go away!"

Jimmy opened the door and stuck his head in. "I *told* you no one would laugh at you, didn't I?"

"You have an interesting Me Tarzan, You Jane approach to the entire male-female relationship, Jimmy. Has anyone ever told you that?"

"Oh, come on—I did the same thing *you* did the day I blew my audition at the Shubert. I just gave you a little pep talk, that's all."

"Yeah. Except yours was physical."

"You know something, Morgan—sometimes it seems that you and I are like an old married couple. No matter what happens between us, we always end up back together again."

"Maybe it's time we start thinking about a divorce, huh?"

He stepped inside the dressing room. "You really mad or what?"

"Let's just put it this way, Jimmy: It's been a hell of a night."

He sat down in the chair next to mine and stretched his legs out. He put his hands behind his head. "I didn't want to see you throw a whole theatrical career away just because you took a little spill onstage."

"I'm glad you did it."

"*What?*"

"You heard me."

"So the divorce is off, huh?"

"I couldn't ever divorce you, Jimmy. You'd be helpless without me."

"Guess you know me pretty well, Morgan."

"I guess after seventeen years there isn't much we *don't* know about each other."

"Let's go home, okay? I think we've had enough show business for one night."

"Jimmy, wait a second. . . . Thanks for covering for me onstage . . . after I fell. . . . Thanks for doing my lines."

"Nothing to it."

"No, really . . . I don't know what I would've done if you hadn't been there. Sometimes it seems like you've been rescuing me from one thing or another all our lives. . . ."

"Come on, Morgan."

"I'm not kidding. You're really not like anyone else I know, Jimmy."

Jimmy wasn't much on compliments, but that was okay with me. He cleared his throat a few times and stood up. He ran his fingers through his hair. "Look . . . Morgan . . . I never know what to say when you talk like that."

"Very simple, Jimmy." I stood up and put my hands on his shoulders. I started steering him out of the dressing room. "Just say goodnight, Gracie."

He shook his head and smiled. "Good*night*, Gracie!"

∽ 13 ⌒

The play ran through Christmas Eve. As soon as the curtain came down, Jimmy and I hit North Avenue and headed back to Glen Ellyn.

"You mind stopping in the village before we go home?" I said. "I have some shopping to do."

"Not your Christmas shopping—"

"Yes, my Christmas shopping. Don't worry; it'll only take a few minutes."

"Gee, there's nothing more heartwarming than the thought of you agonizing for a whole 'few minutes' over what to get me for Christmas, Morgan."

"Jimmy, you're not a method actor, you know. Didn't you leave Scrooge back at Pheasant Run when the play closed?"

He looked at me. "Humbug," he said.

It took us twenty minutes to find a parking place.

"I approve," I said, as we got out of the car. "The snow falling, the decorations, even the crowds. I approve of them."

"You're a real romantic, aren't you, Morgan?"

"And what's wrong with that?"

"Not a thing. Feed the parking meter."

I dragged him up and down Main Street. Into Rystrom's, where I found a beautiful silver filigreed bracelet for my aunt; into Warner's, where I bought a roll of my father's favorite canvas for his oil paintings. At DuJardin's I bought a Nevil Shute book for my mother—she's one of those avid readers who'll read soup-can labels if she doesn't have a book around—and finally, while Jimmy trudged back to the car with my packages, I dashed into Horsley's to buy his present: a light-blue Shetland wool sweater I'd seen in the window.

I looked at my watch when I got in the car. "See? That didn't take too long. An hour and a half, that's all."

"Terrific. Too bad Christmas shopping isn't an Olympic event, Hackett. You'd win a gold medal."

"Just start the car, Ebenezer, okay?"

The Woolfs came over for brunch Christmas morning. For a while *everyone* was crowded into the kitchen: all of us. While my father was piling strips of bacon onto a platter, he broke into a sort of impromptu version of "The Twelve Days of Christmas" and the rest of us joined in. But no one could remember how many lords a-leaping there were, so the song ended up being "White Christmas." My mother and Mrs. Woolf were trying to go for some weird type of harmony while my father and Mr. Woolf did their best to nail down the melody, but none of it was working out too well.

"This is like being trapped inside a Bing Crosby Christmas special," I said to Jimmy. "Let's get out of here." We each took a cup of tea and a hunk of his mother's traditional almond coffee cake into the living room, so we could sit on the floor and eat in front of the fire.

"You know something?" I said. "Now that it's all over, I sort of miss being a theatrical slave. I really learned a lot while I was out there."

Jimmy choked on his tea. "Am I *hearing* right? You *miss* being an apprentice? How can you say that after all the bitching you did about coffee making and errand running?"

"Yeah, Jimmy, but at least I got to hang around the *theater*. I'm really going to miss it, you know?"

"Ben told me he's doing a new play after Christmas. He wants you to read for him."

"Are you *kidding? Really?*"

"Looks like your coffee-making days are over, Morgan. Something we can all be thankful for."

I gave him a little kick. "It'd be nice to get a part of my own," I said. "I told my parents about going on for Robin, but I didn't give them any of the gruesome details. I didn't tell them about falling flat on my face in front of hundreds of people."

"Why not?"

97

"Why not? Because I don't care to advertise my own stupidity, that's why not."

"You put too much emphasis on what people are going to think about you, Morgan."

"Everyone wants respect."

"Not at the expense of their peace of mind."

"You sound like my aunt," I said. I stuffed the last bit of coffee cake into my mouth and brushed the crumbs off my hands. "Why don't you go to medical school and become a psychiatrist? You could become the first tap-dancing shrink at Johns Hopkins."

"I think I'll stick with the theater," he said. "I'm driving into the city tomorrow to talk to this guy at Actors Equity; you want to come with me? There's a chance I might get to do some summer stock up in Wisconsin this year."

"What time are you leaving?"

"Three."

"Okay," I said. "You can drop me off at Second City. I've got to start making up some of the workshops I missed while I was out at Pheasant Run." I looked at him. "You really want to go away and do stock this summer?"

"Sure. It'll be great experience."

"But you can get great experience right here, doing local theater like you did last summer—"

"And the summer before that and the summer before that. This is a step up, Hackett."

"I know," I said.

"Wisconsin isn't exactly Mars, you know. Planes, trains, and busses go there—"

"Are you inviting me up to Wisconsin to visit you?"

"Yes, Morgan, that's exactly what I'm doing."

"Well, I might try to make it," I said. "If I'm not on Broadway by then. Where's my Christmas present?"

He reached into his jacket pocket and pulled out a little envelope and handed it to me. Inside were two theater tickets.

"*Uncommon Women and Others*," Jimmy said. "By Wendy Wasserstein. It's at the Goodman Theater."

"Next week," I said, reading the tickets.

"Oh, by the way: Dinner is included in the present."

"Jimmy, thank you." I reached under the Christmas tree and pulled out his present. "Hope it fits," I said, handing it to him.

He tore off the paper, took the lid off the box. "Very classy," he said, taking the sweater out of the box. He took off his jacket and pulled on the sweater. "I'll wear it tomorrow and impress everyone at Equity."

"Well, wait a second; let me take the tags off, will you?" I made him stand up so I could make sure it fit right, and undid the tags. "You really like it?"

"I really like it."

"Well? Aren't you going to thank me?"

"Thank you."

"That's not exactly what I had in mind, Jimmy."

99

"Come on now, Morgan—"

"I want a Christmas kiss," I said. "And I want it *now*."

"There's no mistletoe."

"Since when do you need mistletoe? I didn't see any mistletoe when you were kissing Robin-the-toothpick!"

"All right! You want a kiss?" He reached down, pulled me to my feet, put his arm around my waist, and suddenly there I was—staring at the ceiling—my head parallel to and nearly touching the floor.

"Didn't I see this in a Fred Astaire movie?" I asked. *"Flying Down to Rio."*

"Jimmy Woolf, if you let go of me and drop me—"

"I know what I'm doing, Hackett." He kissed me, a very nice kiss. Then he let go of me and dropped me on the floor.

"Good friends aren't everything they're cracked up to be," I said.

"Morgan?" my mother called. "Your presence is requested in the kitchen, please."

"Hey, get me another cùp of tea while you're out there," Jimmy said.

"Get it yourself!"

"What was that you were saying about good friends?"

I shook my head and took his cup out to the kitchen. "Look," I said, holding up the theater tickets. "From Jimmy. Next Tuesday."

"Very nice," my mother said. "Loey's on the phone; she wants to talk to you."

"Why isn't she on her way?"

"She's not coming."

"What do you mean she's not coming?"

"What do you mean what do I mean? She's not coming. She's at the hospital and she's busy, so try to keep it short, okay?"

I took the phone from her. "Aunt Lo?"

"Hi, sweetie. Merry Christmas."

"Yeah, Merry Christmas. Mother says you're not coming—"

"Honey, I've got a couple of crises going on here, and I don't want to be too far away from the hospital today."

"Well, don't your patients care if you have a Christmas or not? Why don't they give you the day off?"

"I'm afraid this is just one of those occupational hazards."

"I know I'm being selfish, but I don't care. What are you going to do tonight?"

"Well, Dan's coming over tonight and we're going to open a bottle of champagne I've been saving."

"I'm glad you won't be alone on Christmas."

"Listen, I left your Christmas present with Fay and I want you to open it, okay?"

"Okay . . . but it's just not going to seem like Christmas without you."

"I'll try to make it out there tomorrow——".

"Famous last words!"

She laughed. "You'll see. . . . Honey, I've got to run."

"Okay. See you tomorrow."

The present from my aunt turned out to be a pair of knee-high suede boots.

"Very sexy," Jimmy said.

"Think so?"

"Absolutely."

"That's what I like about you, Jimmy."

"What?"

"Everything," I said.

14

The next afternoon I set my hair on hot rollers and put on a white sweater, jeans, and my new suede boots.

"Jimmy's father left this morning on a business trip," my mother said. She wandered into the bathroom and started rummaging through the medicine chest. "So I thought we'd ask Jimmy and Enid over for dinner."

"Jimmy and I won't be back in time for dinner," I said. "We'll probably grab a bite in the city."

"Do you have enough money?"

"Yes, thank you. . . . What are you looking for?"

"My lipstick. How could I lose my lipstick?"

Jimmy's horn sounded in the driveway. He wouldn't let up on it.

"He's just doing that to drive me crazy," I said. I ran downstairs and opened the front door. "I'm *hurrying*! Keep your shirt on, will you?"

"I've got an appointment, you know!" he hollered. "Traffic's going to be heavy today!"

"I have to do my hair!"

"Do it in the car! Come *on!*"

I grabbed my purse. "Mother, I'm leaving!"

"Have a good time," she said.

"You look like the Cat Woman of Mars," Jimmy said when I got into the car. "You're not going to do that thing with the mirror, are you?"

"You mean this thing?" I turned the rearview mirror so I could see what I was doing while I took the rollers out of my hair.

"Yeah, that thing."

"Well, it's your fault," I said. "Why are you in such a hurry?"

"I want to get there early. It's a compulsion with me."

"I know. Your mother says you were even *born* a week early."

"Well, I had to get into the world early, Morgan, so I'd be here to look after you."

"Ha!" I dumped all the rollers into my purse and started brushing my hair. "God, it's *freezing* in here! Why don't you turn on your heater?"

"It's broken."

"Broken!"

"You cold?"

"Yes, Jimmy, those of us without coats are cold today."

"Why didn't you wear a coat?"

"Because *you* told me to hurry!"

"I told you to hurry, Morgan, not to run out of the house without a coat."

"Well, you did it. You just said I was stupid."

"No. No, I didn't actually come out and *say* it—"

"You implied it, dammit."

"All right now, Morgan, let's not get profane here."

"Jimmy Woolf, I'm getting frostbitten!"

"It's not that cold. You just happen to have a low temperature threshold."

"*You're* the one with the jacket," I said.

"Nag, nag, nag. Take the wheel." I leaned over and steered while he unzipped his jacket and took it off. "Here," he said, tossing it to me. "I understand there are more entertaining ways of warming up a friend, but this is the best I can do while I'm driving—"

"Don't flatter yourself," I said. I put on his jacket and rolled back the cuffs so it would fit me. I looked over at him. "You're wearing your new sweater."

"Uh-huh."

"Jimmy, my hands are cold."

"You can't have my gloves, Hackett."

"Nobody loves me and my hands are cold!"

"God loves you and you can sit on your hands."

"You're so chivalrous."

"I'm trying to drive."

It was really too cold to do much talking. I stuffed my hands into the jacket pockets. When we got into the city, Jimmy drove down North Wells and pulled up alongside Second City. "All right," he said. "Let's see the hands." I pulled my hands out of my pockets and he started rubbing them. "I'll pick you up at five thirty and we'll go eat, okay? If I'm going to be any later, I'll call you."

"Let's eat here in Old Town," I said. "Someplace where they have greasy French fries."

"Anything you want. Your hands warmer now?"

"Yes, thank you."

"See you in about an hour."

"You want your jacket?"

"Keep it."

" 'Bye."

I wrapped his jacket around me and ran into the theater. Patty, this girl from my workshop, was sitting on the lobby stairs tugging off her snow boots.

"Not bad," she said. "Who is he?"

"Who?"

"The guy who just dropped you off."

"Oh . . . he's a friend of mine."

"Your boyfriend?"

"No, we're not— He's just a friend. My best friend, really."

"Your best friend's a *guy*?"

I nodded.

"Definitely weird," Patty said. She pulled off her coat and we started upstairs. "Where've you been? I haven't seen you around lately."

"I was working as an apprentice out at Pheasant Run."

"Yeah? I got a job too. I'm understudying the understudy of the third lead in *The Music Man* over at the Candlelight. I'm supposed to be at rehearsal right now, but I didn't want to miss the party."

"What party?"

"The semester ended last week; we're having a party today."

"I wish I'd known," I said. "I could have brought something."

"Are you *kidding*? You should have seen the food they brought in here a few minutes ago. It looks like they knocked over a couple of hundred delicatessens."

We walked into the theater. Patty headed right for the buffet: a long table set up onstage piled with plates of meats and cheeses and breads, bowls filled with chips and dips, crackers and pretzels. I checked my watch. I wanted to be someplace else. *Anyplace* else. I was just really lousy at party mingling unless I had someone like Jimmy beside me to help me break the ice. I was beginning to wish I'd gone with him to Equity and waited for him in the car, heater or no heater.

"Morgan," I heard someone say, "welcome back." I turned around. The director of my workshop walked over to me and handed me a glass of wine. "I understand you've been apprenticing out at Pheasant Run, huh?"

"Yeah, how'd you know?"

"Ben Kubelsky's a friend of mine. You know something? My whole workshop's defecting. First you. Then

Patty. She's at the Candlelight for six weeks. Then Marnie over there—she's at the Goodman this month in *Uncommon Women and Others*."

"Really? My friend and I have tickets next Tuesday."

"It's good to have you back, Morgan. Our new semester starts next month; don't forget."

"I won't. Thanks."

I walked around sipping wine, nibbling on crackers, smiling at people, and trying to act like I was having a hell of a time. I managed to spend a whole hour in the middle of a party all by myself, which I decided was pretty pathetic. For my self-esteem alone I felt I had to take a crack at being sociable before I left. I walked up to the buffet table to talk to Patty and tried to think up some typical party talk.

"How was your Christmas?" I asked.

I think I shifted gears much too fast for her, because she gave me a blank stare and dropped her Dorito chip into the guacamole.

"Oh!" she said. "Christmas. . . . See, my boyfriend and I don't celebrate Christmas because it's so crass and commercial and everything. We're thinking of starting our own religion. If we can find enough people."

"Uh-huh," I said. I set my wine glass down; it was definitely time to leave.

For the first time in history Jimmy was late picking me up. I had to stand out there on North Wells in the bitter cold, in the dark. I pulled the collar of Jimmy's jacket up around my neck and walked back and forth in front of the theater—I learned a long time ago it's not a good idea to remain stationary for any length of time in the city. It has to do with my theory about weirdos finding it harder to hit a moving target. After half an hour I was mad enough at Jimmy and cold enough to go back into the theater and call him at Actors Equity. I didn't care if they were offering him the deal of a lifetime. I ran up the stairs and went back behind the bar and looked up the number in the phone book. My fingers were so numb, I actually had to let them thaw out a little before I could put any change in the pay phone and dial.

"Actors Equity," a woman said. "Can I help you?"

"Uh, yeah. . . . I'd like to know if Jimmy Woolf is still there. He had a four forty-five appointment—"

"I know," the woman said. "We've been trying to reach him."

"Reach him. . . ."

"He never showed up."

"But he left for there over an hour and a half ago."

"Maybe he had car trouble. When you see him, will you ask him to give us a call? We can only hold that summer-stock job open one more day."

"I'll tell him," I said. "Thanks."

I went back outside. It wasn't like Jimmy not to call. Even if he'd had car trouble—which was certainly possible the way that old heap of his kept falling apart—

he would have found a way to get to a phone. It was city streets all the way fro· . Old Town to the Loop, and if Jimmy's car had s. pped in the middle of all that traffic, someone would have called a tow truck. And how long would it take a tow truck to reach him? Fifteen minutes? Maybe twenty? I looked at my watch and decided to give him another hour. Then I'd definitely call someone. His mother. Or the police. I walked back and forth in front of the theater. I stood by the curb and looked down North Wells. I must have stood there a long time. Long enough for my fingers and toes to get numb, long enough to count over two hundred cars. And my eyes tricked me: Three times I was sure I saw Jimmy's MG, three times I was wrong. He never came, and my mind turned to practical matters: How would I get home? I had a little cash on me, but not enough for cab and train fare. I was thinking about going inside and calling my aunt when a car pulled right up beside me and jerked to a stop. It was our car, and my mother was driving. She reached over and opened the door.

"You must be frozen," she said. "Get in, darling."

"But Jimmy—"

"I know. I'll tell you all about it. Get in." So I got in and barely had a chance to slam the door shut before my mother's foot went down on the accelerator.

"Listen to me now," she said in a tone of measured calm. "Jimmy's been hurt. There was an accident—"

I looked at her. "What do you mean *hurt*?"

"There was a car accident. We're still not sure how bad it was—"

"What happened? He's all right, isn't he?"

"We just don't know. Your aunt's in the emergency room right now trying to find out what's going on—"

"But I don't *understand*!" I said. "He's a careful driver! He's always been such a careful driver!"

"The police said the other driver had been drinking. Apparently he jumped lanes and skidded into Jimmy's car—"

"What did Aunt Lo say? Jimmy's not unconscious, is he?"

"Darling, I didn't have time to talk to her. I dropped Enid off at the hospital and came right over here to pick you up."

I looked down at my hands. They were shaking. "I knew something was wrong . . . when he didn't come."

"Oh, dear God," my mother said. "I was just . . . I was just thinking how glad I was you weren't riding with him when it happened."

⌒ 15 ⌒

"I remember something Mrs. Woolf said to me once," I said to my mother. She wasn't even listening. She was hurrying—running ahead of me—taking the hospital steps two at a time. "Mother, will you *wait*? I want to tell you something—"

"Now?"

"It's important. I was talking to Mrs. Woolf—"

"Oh, damn, I'm all turned around," my mother said. She stopped just inside the hospital doors. "Which way is Emergency?"

"It's downstairs. We have to take the elevator."

"I must be losing my mind," my mother said. We went over to the elevators, and she punched the down button and we waited.

"Anyway," I said, "she was talking about Jimmy—"

"Who was?"

"Mrs. Woolf. Mrs. Woolf and I were talking about Jimmy once," I said. "And she told me Jimmy always bounces back."

"Oh . . . Morgan . . ."

"I'm just telling you what she said."

We took the elevator downstairs and hurried down the hall. I was getting a stitch in my side from walking so fast. We passed a lounge Jimmy and I had played cards in while we waited to take my aunt to dinner one night. He had beaten me roundly—he always did. I still owed him $4.80.

We turned a corner. My aunt was sitting there holding Mrs. Woolf's hands and talking to her. I knew by the way she was talking that Jimmy was dead. Nobody had to tell me.

"No," my mother said. "Oh, no . . ."

She went over and put her arms around Mrs. Woolf and I sort of shuffled off into the background. I didn't understand. I didn't know what to do. Jimmy dead? I had just seen him a few hours earlier. I was still wearing his jacket. How could he be dead? I turned around and walked back down the hall. I didn't know where I was going—I was just automatically walking. I went around a corner and bumped into a nurse—my aunt's friend, Mrs. Getz. She tried to put her arm around my shoulders, but I pulled away and kept walking. I went into the lounge and sat down on a couch and tried to make my hands stop shaking and my heart slow down. I couldn't think.

Suddenly I felt my aunt's hand on the back of my neck. "I've been looking for you," she said.

"I didn't want anyone to see me like this." I didn't like not being in control. I know I place too much importance on the way I appear to the outside world, and I keep things inside too much. I don't like to give pieces of myself away. There are very few people I'm willing to do that for. Jimmy was one. My aunt is one.

I looked up at her. She seemed very concerned. "I'll get through this," I said. "I'll handle it."

"Of course you will."

My mother walked into the lounge and stopped and looked at me. Her mascara had run and made black half-moons under her eyes. I wanted to cry too, but I couldn't. It was like there was a curtain of glass between the part of my brain that knew Jimmy was dead and the part that could feel anything about it.

"You know, don't you?"

"Yes," I said.

"Are you all right?"

"Yes," I said. I pushed my hands down into my pockets so no one would see them shaking.

"I think we'll quiet you down a little," my aunt said. "Betty?" She looked across the hall to Mrs. Getz. "I want to get ten milligrams of diazepam i.m. into Morgan."

"I'll go ask one of the emergency room nurses for it," Mrs. Getz said.

My mother sat down in a chair and put her head in her hands. "Enid's talking long distance to Jack," she said. "He's catching a late flight home from Cleveland, and I'm going to stay with her until he gets here."

"Will she be all right?"

"Enid? I don't know. I don't see how she's going to live through this, I honestly don't."

"I want to know how it happened," I said. "I want to know how he died."

"Oh, Morgan, *no*," my mother said.

"I want to KNOW!"

My aunt didn't say anything right away. She sat down on the couch and looked at me. "Jimmy was thrown about a hundred feet from his car. He was in a coma when they brought him in, and he never regained consciousness. He died of massive head injuries."

"He was in a coma? When did he die?"

"About fifteen minutes ago."

"Did you see him?"

"I was right there," my aunt said. "I held his hand."

"Where is he now?" I asked. "The body, I mean. Where is it?"

My mother took a bunched-up Kleenex out of her purse and blew her nose. She was crying again. "Loey . . . why is she *doing* this?"

"I have to know," I whispered to my aunt. "Where is he?"

"The body is in the emergency room," she said. "The mortuary is going to pick it up."

"Oh."

Mrs. Getz walked into the lounge and handed my aunt a capped hypodermic needle. I think I was a little nuts.

"I'm not going to take it off," I said.

My mother stopped sniffling and looked at me blankly. "Take what off?"

"The jacket," I said. "It's Jimmy's. I'm not going to take it off."

My mother looked from me to my aunt. There was a mixture of confusion and worry in her face.

"It hasn't caught up with her yet," my aunt said. She unbuttoned the cuff of Jimmy's jacket and pushed up the sleeve. "You don't have to take off his jacket until you want to, honey."

"My *heart*," I said. "I can feel my *heart*."

"I'm going to give you some sedation," my aunt said, "and it's going to make your heart stop pounding . . . and calm you down so the shaking will stop." She tore open this little packet Mrs. Getz handed her and took out an alcohol pad and swabbed my arm.

"I don't want that," I said. I looked at my aunt. "I mean it. I don't want a shot."

"I'm sorry, sweetie—this is something you just don't have any choice about." She uncapped the needle and squirted a little fountain of liquid into the air. "Okay? It only hurts for a second." She brought the needle down against my arm. I looked away. Damn you, Jimmy, I thought. Where are you and your lousy jokes when I need you? I felt a sharp sting, then bit by bit the shaking stopped. My heart slowed. I was able to breathe and see.

"It feels funny," I said. "Like I'm . . . floating or something."

"Mm-hmm," my aunt said. She handed the empty hypodermic needle to Mrs. Getz and looked at me. "Are you feeling a little sleepy yet?"

"Sort of."

"I'm going to take you home with me tonight, all right?" She pulled the sleeve of Jimmy's jacket down and buttoned the cuff at my wrist. "Betty . . . would you have someone bring my car around?"

"Of course," Mrs. Getz said.

My aunt put her arms around me and pulled me against her white coat. "Fay, do you want me to have someone drive you and Enid home?"

"No—we'll be all right." My mother cleared her throat. I could tell she was trying really hard to pull herself together. "Loey . . . she's okay, isn't she? For tonight, I mean."

". . . a walloping dose of a tranquilizer . . . she'll sleep through the night . . ."

"And then?"

". . . rough . . . for Enid, too . . ."

I could barely sort out what they were saying. I tried hard to focus on my mother, tried hard to concentrate.

". . . should be getting back to Enid," my mother said. She stood up and came over and kissed me.

"Fay . . . try not to worry. . . . I'll call you in the morning. . . ."

My mother nodded. I must have slept: The next thing I knew, my aunt was shifting me from her shoulder, my mother was gone, and Mrs. Getz was standing there holding my aunt's coat and medical bag and purse.

"Okay, come on," my aunt said. "Let's go home." She took her coat from Mrs. Getz and threw it over my shoulders.

"I can't walk," I said. "My legs feel funny."

"Make your knees stiff," my aunt said. "Come on now. . . . Mrs. Getz and I have got you. . . ." We walked out of the hospital and up some steps to the car. "Betty, one more thing," my aunt said. "Give my housekeeper a call and tell her we're on the way."

"I'll call her right away," Mrs. Getz said. She opened the door, and I slid onto the front seat while my aunt went around and got in on the other side.

"Aunt Lo, are those new?" I asked. "Your earrings— did you get them for Christmas?"

"Mm-hmm." She reached over and pulled my seat belt across me and buckled it.

"Jimmy gave me tickets for a play next Tuesday," I said. "What should I do with them?"

"Oh, honey." She started the car. "Don't worry about it now."

Mrs. Rassin came out to the car as soon as we pulled into the drive. She opened the door on my side, and I could see her eyes were red rimmed and watery.

"Dr. Hackett . . . I just can't believe this has happened."

"I know," my aunt said. "Give me a hand here, will you?"

"Is she all right?"

"A little unsteady," my aunt said. "I sedated her. Is the bed in the guest room made up?"

"Yes," Mrs. Rassin said.

The covers on the bed were turned back. My aunt sat me down on the bed and pulled her coat off my shoulders.

"Aunt Lo . . . Jimmy's really dead?"

"Yes, honey."

"You're a doctor," I said. "You've seen people die before."

"Yes."

"Do you ever get used to it?"

"No." She bent down and unzipped my boots and pulled them off.

"Dr. Hackett," Mrs. Rassin said, "I just put some coffee on."

"How about something a little stronger?"

"I'll get you a drink."

"Come on, lie back," my aunt said. She pushed me down against the pillows. "I want you to give that shot a chance to work."

"I don't feel sad or anything," I said. "Is that wrong?"

"No, honey, it's not wrong."

"I don't feel anything at all."

Everyone had gone to pieces except me. Mrs. Woolf and my mother and Mrs. Rassin. Even my aunt. As soon as she pulled the covers up around me, she turned out the light and sat down on the bed. I saw the flare from her cigarette lighter.

She was smoking again.

Part Two

∽ 16 ⌒

I couldn't figure out what I was doing in my aunt's guest room. I really didn't connect why I was there, not until I rolled over onto my arm and it hurt and I remembered the shot my aunt had given me and why.

"How do you feel?" my aunt asked. She sat down on the bed and lit a cigarette. She was wearing a pair of jeans and a sweatshirt, just like it was an ordinary day.

"What happened to the other driver?" I asked. "Was he killed too?"

Killed was the word for it. Jimmy didn't die, he wouldn't do that to me, he was killed.

"The other driver wasn't even hurt," my aunt said. "He was charged with reckless homicide, and dammit, he's already out on bail."

"What happens now?" I said. "I mean . . . I guess there'll be a funeral—"

"Day after tomorrow."

I took a deep breath.

"I'm okay," I said, and my aunt smiled and touched

my face. I don't think she believed me. "What was that," I said. "You know . . . that shot you gave me last night. What was it?"

"Valium."

"I didn't need it," I said. "I tried to tell you I was all right. I tried to tell you I could handle this."

My aunt squinted at me and took a drag on her cigarette. She didn't say anything.

My father drove in that afternoon to pick me up. My aunt bundled up and went out to the car to meet him. I watched them from the kitchen window. His arm went around my aunt's shoulders, his head was down. My guess was confirmed when they walked into the kitchen: He was crying.

"How you doing?" he asked.

"Okay. I'm almost ready." He put his arms around me, but it was like I didn't even feel his hug. "You don't look too good," I said.

"Well, I was up all night with Jack," my father said. "Poor Jack. . . .When he got off the plane, he was drunk and crying and full of regrets. He kept talking about all the things he never had a chance to tell Jimmy . . . all the things they'd never done together."

I thought maybe my father was going to break down. I couldn't stand it. I sat at the kitchen table and pulled my boots on. "Is Mother with Mrs. Woolf?"

"She's helping Enid talk to the minister."

"Minister!" I said. "What minister? The Woolfs never go to church."

"They're Presbyterian, I think," my father said. "Anyway, this minister is setting up the arrangements—"

"What arrangements?"

"For the funeral."

"Oh."

"Enid thought you might want to say something at the service," my father said.

"Say something . . . what . . . you mean like a eulogy or something?"

"No, nothing like that. She thought you could read a poem that meant something to Jimmy—she says he liked Carl Sandburg."

"You didn't tell her I'd do it, did you?"

"No, of course not," my father said.

"Because I don't think I could. Get up in front of all those people and—I just don't think I could do it."

"You don't have to," my father said. "It was just an idea, that's all. Are you going to be warm enough in that?"

I was still wearing Jimmy's jacket. I pulled up the collar and nodded. Before I went out the door, my aunt took off her long white muffler and wrapped it around my neck. "I'm driving out for the funeral," she said. "But if you need anything before then—even if you just want to talk—you can reach me here or at the hospital."

"I know," I said. "I'll be all right."

My aunt and my father looked at each other, and my father put his hands on my shoulders. "Let's get going," he said. "We've got a long drive ahead."

On the way home I said to my father, "Aunt Lo's waiting for me to fall apart, and I'm not going to."

"Would it be so terrible," my father said, "if you fell apart a little?"

"Sometimes you and Aunt Lo sound exactly alike."

"I guess we do. Sometimes."

When we got home, I took off Jimmy's jacket, folded it, and put it into the garbage can.

"You don't have to, you know, Morgan," my father said. "That's Jimmy's jacket, isn't it?"

"Yes," I said. "But it reminds me of last night . . . of the accident. . . . I don't know. I just think it would be kind of morbid to hang on to it." And I dropped the lid onto the can.

I couldn't sleep that night. Long after my parents were in bed, I lay on my back and stared at the ceiling and thought: *Well, he's dead.* I couldn't stop thinking about Jimmy, thrown a hundred feet from his car. Jimmy, who died of massive head injuries. Jimmy, who never even knew my aunt was standing right there beside him in the emergency room holding his hand.

I swung my legs over the edge of the bed and sat there for a few minutes, listening to my heart pound.

I wasn't stupid—I knew Jimmy was dead—but I felt like I had to talk to him. I did what I thought was the next-best thing: I went out by the garage and pulled Jimmy's jacket out of the garbage can. When I got upstairs, I didn't even wait for it to thaw out. I put it on, zipped it up, and got back into bed.

In the morning I would roll it up and hide it under my mattress. For now it was all right: It was like having Jimmy's arms wrapped around me.

For now, that was enough.

My mother bought me a dark dress for the funeral. I didn't try it on until right before we left for the service, which was when I discovered it was way too big for me.

"Damn," my mother said. "I knew I should have gotten a smaller size."

"I'll have my coat on," I said. "No one will see it."

"I wish you'd eat something before we leave. . . . God, I still can't believe he's gone—"

"He's not *gone,*" I said. "Why do people always *say* that? Jimmy's not gone. He's dead."

My mother looked at me. "Are you all right? I know how awful this is for you."

"What day is it? Monday or Tuesday?"

"Tuesday."

"That play Jimmy gave me tickets for," I said. "It's tonight."

"Morgan, you're not thinking of going into the city tonight—"

"No," I said. "No, of course not." But I couldn't

stop thinking about the play, and about two seats in the tenth row at the Goodman that would be empty that night.

I was okay for a while. I was okay during the ride downtown. It really was a beautiful day, clear and cold: a day for sledding or skating, not for burying my best and only friend. When we got downtown, we parked on one of the streets next to the church. We parked right next to my aunt's car.

"Did I tell you?" I said. "She's smoking again."

"Who is?" my father asked.

"Aunt Lo. She started smoking again."

"Well," he said. "This is a hard time for all of us."

"But she's a doctor. She should know better."

"Being a doctor doesn't make death easier to cope with."

I hadn't thought of it like that. To me, *I* was the only one affected by Jimmy's death, but as we walked to the church, I saw the others: his first dance teacher, actors who had worked with him in those summer musicals he did. I saw his grandparents and parents. Mrs. Woolf looked absolutely destroyed.

"I can't go in," I said.

"What's wrong?" my mother asked.

"I'm going back to the car."

"Oh . . . Morgan."

"Jimmy wasn't religious, and neither am I."

"It would mean something to Enid, your being there."

"I'm sorry," I said. "I just—I don't feel very good." I turned around and cut across the snowy yard to the street. I was cold and sweating, and with each step I took, my vision seemed to darken and narrow. If Jimmy had been by my side, he would have whispered something funny and inappropriate about funerals. Jimmy was the person who helped me through the rough spots. Without him who would I go through life laughing with?

The car door was locked. I figured my options: stay out in the cold or go inside to the funeral. I chose the cold.

"This is wonderful skating weather," I heard my father say. "When I was your age, your aunt and I spent the entire winter skating down at Lake Ellyn. She used to be quite an ice skater—did you know that?"

I looked at the church. "I remember coming here with Jimmy once," I said. "For Sunday school. They told us Bible stories and we had crackers and juice."

I felt his hand touch mine. "Morgan . . ."

I looked at him. "I had to get out of there. I saw Mrs. Woolf and I couldn't go in."

"Do you want to go home?"

"Yes," I said.

"Here." He handed me the car keys. "We'll get a ride home with Loey."

"I thought you came out here to talk me into going to the funeral."

"I wouldn't do that," my father said. "Be careful, okay? The streets are a little icy."

"I know it's wrong to ditch Jimmy's funeral. . . . I know I'm letting Mrs. Woolf down—"

My father gave my hand a squeeze. "Enid's not the one you're letting down, kiddo."

I didn't want to hear him. I got in and started the car. I knew he meant I was letting myself down, but how was going to the funeral going to help me? Jimmy was dead, whether I went to the funeral or not.

18

I went back to school the next Monday. I got up early that morning, grabbed a cup of coffee, went upstairs to wind my hair on rollers. My mother came into the bathroom while I was putting on my makeup.

"How long have you been up?" she asked.

"I don't know. A little while."

"It wouldn't hurt you to take a few more days to catch up on your rest; I know you haven't been sleeping well—"

"I *want* to go back," I said. "I just . . . I feel like if I can just get back into a routine, then maybe I'll start feeling normal again."

"I know."

"Are you going over to Mrs. Woolf's today?"

"I'm taking her down to a meeting at the church."

"A meeting? What kind of meeting?"

"It's a support group for parents who've lost a child."

"Mrs. Woolf didn't *lose* Jimmy," I said. "He didn't disappear. He died."

"It seems less painful to say it the other way."

"Maybe," I said. "But it means the same thing."

All the colors had drained from the earth. I walked alone to school for the first time ever, and one of the first things I saw when I walked into the building was the vice principal cleaning out Jimmy's locker, tossing his books and things into a green Hefty bag.

"Those things," I said. "You're not throwing those things out, are you?"

"No, no, nothing like that," the vice principal said. "But we need this locker. A lot of the freshmen are sharing lockers, and this student's not coming back—"

"But his *things*," I said. "What are you going to do with his things?"

"Send them to his new school, I guess."

"His new school . . ."

"He was transferred to a new school over the holidays."

"He was *killed*," I said. "There was a car accident over the holidays and he was *killed*."

"Are you sure?" He took a slip of paper from his pocket and looked at it. "James Woolf?"

"Yes. Jimmy Woolf. He was killed."

"You were a friend of his?"

"Yes," I said.

"Well," he said. "I didn't know about the accident. I *am* sorry."

❊   ❊   ❊

"Hey," Jody whispered at the beginning of English. "Look. Mrs. Klein got her hair cut. It makes her look about a hundred years younger, don't you think?"

"Yeah," I said.

"I think she had a tint job, too." She looked over at me. "Oh . . . hey, Morgan . . . I heard about Jimmy. . . . It's really awful, isn't it?"

"Yes," I said. "It really is awful."

"Were you—you weren't in the accident too, were you?"

I cleared my throat. "No. It happened after he dropped me off at my acting workshop. He dropped me off, and I guess . . . I guess it happened not too long after that."

"I'm sorry; I didn't mean to—"

"I know. It's okay. I know." I tried to smile, but I couldn't. Inside, I could feel the adrenaline kick in; my heart started pounding. Pounding hard. I didn't understand what was happening to me.

"Morgan," I heard Mrs. Klein say, "Morgan, are you all right? You don't look—"

"Excuse me," I said. "I don't feel very good." I stood up and walked out of class. Just like that. It was like my body had forgotten how to breathe. I knew my heart couldn't forget how to beat, but couldn't it stop? Jimmy's had. I ran down the hall to the washroom and splashed cold water on my face. It didn't help any: I actually thought I was dying.

"Hey," I heard Jody say. "Hey, are you all right?"

"No," I said. "I think I'm having a heart attack."

"You're too young to have a heart attack."

"Tell me about it."

"Do you want me to get the nurse?"

"She's not here on Mondays."

"Here," Jody said. She opened the door to one of the stalls. "I know it's not a chair or a couch, but at least it's a place to sit down." I went in and sat down on the john. My heart wasn't pounding as hard. "You know, the nurse never does anything anyway," Jody said. "I had this terrible headache once, and she couldn't even give me aspirin. It's against the law or something."

"I know," I said.

"I never should have asked you about it. I'm really sorry."

I took a deep breath. "No, it's okay."

"I know how close you and Jimmy were; I used to see you guys walking around the halls together, talking and laughing."

I looked up at her.

"I guess you must really miss him," Jody said.

"Yeah," I said. "I really do."

After school I went back to Mrs. Klein's class to retrieve my books. They were stacked neatly on a corner of her desk.

"Are you feeling all right now?" she asked.

"Yes, thanks."

"Jody mentioned about the boy who died—he was a friend of yours, wasn't he?"

"Yes."

"I'm sure you're going through a very rough time right now. I want you to know how sorry I am."

Everyone extending their sympathies to me made me feel like I was a widow or something, and I guess in a way I was. I went to my locker and got out my jacket and boots and put them on by the Circle Drive entrance. I kept glancing down the hill at the traffic. In the back of my head I was waiting for Jimmy's red MG to drive up the hill and pull around by the front door the way it always did, and when I realized what I was doing, I punished myself by walking all the way home in the cold with my jacket flapping open.

"Are you crazy?" my mother said when I came up the walk. "Do you want to catch pneumonia?"

"No, I don't want to catch pneumonia, and yes, maybe I'm crazy."

"Morgan—don't . . ."

"How did Mrs. Woolf do at her meeting?"

"Well, she said it helps . . . being with other people who've been through the same thing. . . . How was school?"

"I don't know." She pushed the door wide open for me, and I ducked inside, out of the cold. "Jimmy and I didn't have a single class together, but we saw each other during the day: between classes . . . at lunch . . . and he always brought me home after school."

"I know," my mother said. "I looked out the window

a few minutes ago; I half expected to see the two of you pull up in his MG."

I took off my jacket and shook the snow off it. "The night Jimmy was killed. What time did it happen? The accident, I mean."

"Why?"

"I just . . . I need to know. What time did it happen, exactly?"

"Uh . . . I think the police said it happened about four thirty. There were people who saw it—they called an ambulance and tried to help."

"Jimmy dropped me off right at four thirty," I said. "God! A minute or two later and—" I looked at my mother. "It could have been *me*, too. It almost *was*. It could have been *me*."

"What happened to Jimmy was tragic," my mother said. She put her hands on my shoulders and looked at me. "But I'm not sorry he dropped you off when he did."

My heart skipped a couple of beats. I sat down on the stairs and tried to stay calm. My mother sat down beside me and put her arm around me.

"My God, you're shaking," she said. "Listen to me: It was an accident. A terrible, random accident."

I couldn't talk. I sat there with my mother for a long time. I knew what she had said was true: Jimmy's death was a random event; but that didn't quiet my heart. Why Jimmy?

Why not *me*?

19

My father was waiting for me out on Circle Drive the next day after school. I knew he was there even before I saw him, because I could hear one of his favorite Bach concertos blaring from the car's tape deck. The only classical music in a sea of acid rock.

He smiled when he saw me and opened the door. "Hop in," he said.

I got in and threw my books onto the backseat. "How come you're here?" I asked.

"Do I need a reason to pick up my favorite daughter?"

"I *have* to be your favorite daughter. I'm your *only* daughter."

"A technicality. Don't forget your seat belt." I buckled my seat belt, and my father began easing the car down the icy hill and into the traffic on Crescent. "You got a call from that guy out at Pheasant Run this afternoon," my father said. "What's-his-name."

"Kubelsky. Ben Kubelsky."

"Right. He's holding an audition in about an hour for

138

another children's play, and he wants you to read for him."

"Oh."

"Do you want to do it?"

"I don't know. I guess so. Yeah."

"I'll run you out there."

"I don't know how long it'll take. You could miss a whole afternoon of painting."

"What makes you think I'm painting today?"

"Look at your jeans!" My father's jeans were covered with an entire spectrum of oil paint, a sure sign he was in the middle of a painting.

He looked down at himself and laughed. "Okay. Maybe you *should* drop me off at home. I'm not dressed to go wandering around a fancy place like Pheasant Run."

"What are you working on now?"

"The gallery wants me to finish my front-porch series for the opening next week."

"I like your front porches, but I think I like your paintings of people the best."

"Yeah . . . you know something? One of these days I'm going to do a group portrait of your mother, your aunt, and you. I'm going to call it *The Women Who Run My Life*."

"Very funny!"

"Know what?" my father said. "It's nice to see you smile."

He reached over and squeezed my hand.

* * *

I dropped my father at home and drove on to Pheasant Run. I found Ben in the empty theater, setting up folding chairs around a couple of tables that had been pushed together.

"Morgan, hi," he said. "Right on time. Why don't you have a seat; the rest of the gang should be here in a few minutes."

I sat down. I picked up a script and looked through it. "What's the play?"

"The Goose That Laid the Golden Egg," Ben said. "Not exactly Shakespeare, is it? Oh, Morgan . . . before everyone else gets here . . . I want to talk to you about something." He sat down across from me. "I almost didn't call you about the audition. I wasn't sure how you'd feel about trying out for a play Jimmy was supposed to be in—"

"Oh," I said. "No . . . I want to do it."

"You know, I heard about it on the radio," Ben said. "About Jimmy. Only I didn't think it was the same James Woolf. Hell, you hear about traffic fatalities all the time, don't you? You never think it's going to happen to someone you know. It was a drunk driver, wasn't it?"

I flipped through page after page of the script. "Yeah," I said. "Yeah. It was a drunk driver."

"God, when I think about the *career* that boy had ahead of him . . ."

"Yeah, I know," I said. "I know."

*   *   *

About thirty people finally showed up for the audition. Ben called two or three at a time to read for him; everyone else studied their scripts or had coffee or just got together in small groups to talk. I felt a little out of place. Besides Ben, the only other person I knew there was Robin-the-toothpick, and I just couldn't bring myself to go over to her and hear yet another "I'm sorry he's dead" speech. I ended up sitting off to the side of the stage in a quiet corner. I opened the script and tried to shut out everything and concentrate on what I was reading.

"Robin!" I heard someone call. I looked up. This young guy jumped up onstage and sat down next to Robin. He had a script in his hand. "What part are you reading for?"

"The crying princess."

"I'd like to try out for the male lead, but I know that guy'll get it; he always does."

"What guy?"

"The dancer . . . you know, the one who does all the musicals . . . Jimmy something."

"God, you didn't *hear* about that?"

"About what?"

"He was killed right after Christmas."

"Shit, are you *kidding*?"

"No, I'm not kidding."

"You sure we're talking about the same guy? Jimmy something, right? That tall guy who does all the musicals?"

"Yeah, Jimmy Woolf."

"Jesus, what happened?"

"Killed by a drunk driver."

"Christ . . . maybe I have a chance at the lead after all."

I looked down at my script. *The Goose That Laid the Golden Egg.* Suddenly the whole thing seemed pretty silly. I stood up. I made myself go over to Ben; I wasn't going to just run out like I had in Mrs. Klein's class.

"Ben . . . I think maybe it's too soon for me," I said. "Would you call me for the next play?"

"Oh . . . sure, dear. I'll call you. Take care." I turned around and took a shortcut through the backstage area. I pushed the stage door open and clanked down the same steps Jimmy had that night he'd come after me: the night we did the play together.

I got in the car and started it. On the way home I spotted a small red car up ahead. I couldn't even tell if it was an MG, but I had to find out. I had to see who was driving it. I did a totally insane thing: hit the accelerator and took off after that car like I was Alice going after the White Rabbit. I broke the speed limit all the way to Glen Ellyn. When I got close enough, I saw that the car wasn't an MG, it was a Triumph. The driver wasn't Jimmy, just some girl about my age who flicked her hair away from her face like she didn't have a care in the world.

When I pulled into our driveway, I took a good long look at myself in the rearview mirror.

"You," I said, "are crazy."

I had trouble sleeping that night. I got out of bed and went downstairs and turned on the television, but all I could find was a bunch of depressing news on one channel and Women's Championship Wrestling on the other.

"I thought I heard you up," my mother said. She came over to the couch and sat down next to me. "What happened at the theater today? You didn't say much when you got home."

"God, I must have been crazy. . . . I don't know *why* I thought I could just go out there like nothing's happened and try out for some stupid play. . . ."

"It's going to take a while, don't you think?"

"I guess. Yeah."

"Do you want to talk about it?"

"I just want to sit here for a little while."

"How about some company, then? What's on television?"

"Women's wrestling."

"I don't think we're *that* desperate!" my mother said. "Why don't I read to you, okay? I'll get the Nevil Shute book you gave me for Christmas; I haven't started it yet."

"You don't have to stay up with me."

"Mothers are *supposed* to stay up with their insomniac children. If they didn't, they could be drummed out of the Mothers' Union. You wouldn't want *that* to happen, would you?"

"Who, me? No. Never."

"Good."

I didn't know it then, but that was just the first of many sleepless nights for me. And my mother and father were always there: As soon as I got out of bed, some weird type of parent radar would activate, and one of them would follow me downstairs. They wouldn't let me sit alone and watch television. Instead, they took turns staying up with me and reading to me: a book, a newspaper, a magazine. Sometimes we'd work crossword puzzles. After a week or so we'd finished the Nevil Shute book, gone through seven *Chicago Tribunes*, two *Time* magazines, and at least ten crossword puzzles. I got so I liked the crossword puzzles best. As my mother put it at three thirty one morning: "You may not be getting much sleep, but your vocabulary's really expanding. What's a three-letter word for a flightless Australian bird?"

I pulled the curtains aside and stared out into the night. "Emu," I said.

20

"Loey called this afternoon," my mother said Friday after school. "She wants you to come for dinner and stay over tonight."

"Oh . . ."

"Do you want to go? Your dad's taking his paintings in to the gallery for the opening tomorrow; he said he'll drop you off at the hospital—"

"I don't know. . . ."

"Come on, cutie ," my father said. He stood in the doorway with a crated painting in his hands. "Ride in with me, at least. Keep me company."

I thought about driving into the city with my father. I thought about getting away, seeing my aunt, and sinking down into that antique four-poster in her guest room. I'd never had any trouble sleeping in that bed.

"I'll go throw some clothes into my duffel bag," I said.

We were on our way by four thirty and downtown in the Loop by six.

"I hate winter in the city after the Christmas decorations come down," I said. "Everything looks so bleak and depressing."

"Have to have winter before you can have spring."

I looked at him.

"Just an observation, kiddo. How'd it go last night? Did you sleep at all?"

"No. I'm thinking of entering the Miss Teenage Zombie of America Contest."

"Yeah," my father said. "I guess you'd win the title if you entered."

He drove down East Superior and swung around in front of the hospital. "I'll be up in a minute; I have to find a place to park—"

"You're coming in?"

"Just for a minute. I want to say hi to Loey."

I grabbed my duffel bag. "Park carefully," I said.

I took the elevator up to the psych floor. Mrs. Getz was at the nurses' station. So was Rosalie, that student nurse Jimmy had teased the day I'd come to get my ears pierced.

"Hi, Mrs. Getz," I said. "Is my aunt around?"

"Let me see if she's in her office," Mrs. Getz said. She picked up the phone. Rosalie smiled at me.

"Dr. Hackett's niece, right?"

"Yeah, that's right."

"I thought I remembered you. Where's your friend?"

I just stared at her.

"You know," she said. "The guy you were with that day?"

"Oh," I said. "He's a dancer and he's out on tour now."

"A *dancer*," Rosalie said. "That's really something."

"Yes," I said. "Isn't it?" I don't know why I lied to Rosalie, except it sort of made Jimmy seem alive again. In Rosalie's mind he was out on tour, dancing somewhere.

"You can go on into your aunt's office now, Morgan," Mrs. Getz said.

"Thanks, Mrs. Getz."

My aunt was sitting on the edge of her desk talking on the phone when I walked in. She was wearing this very pretty blue paisley skirt, which I unfortunately couldn't see much of because her white coat covered most of it up.

"Hi," I said.

She covered the mouthpiece with her hand. "That's not a *real* greeting," she said to me. She held out her arm and I went over to her and she gave me this big hug. It's very nice there are people in this world who are so happy to see you they want to hug you. "Tomorrow at eight," she said into the phone. "Semiformal, I guess. . . . Okay. . . . I'll see you at the gallery, then. 'Bye." She hung up and looked at me. "Some of my friends are coming to your dad's opening tomorrow night."

"He'll like that," I said. I sat down in the chair facing her desk. I put the duffel bag in my lap. "He'll be up in a minute to say hi."

"Good." She reached for her pack of Tareytons. "What's going on with you, hmm? You look a little run-down."

"I don't know." I started tugging at the zipper on my duffel bag. "I don't know what's going on with me, exactly."

I felt her hand on my forehead. "Would you let me take you down to one of the examination rooms and check you over?"

I looked at her. "Don't you ever stop being a doctor?"

She smiled and lit her cigarette. "Nope."

"I'm still going through stuff right now. I'll be okay."

There was a knock on the door. My father opened it and walked over to my aunt and gave her a quick kiss on the cheek. "Hi. I'm triple-parked—I can't stay long; I just wanted to talk to you about something." He sat on the arm of the chair I was sitting in and looked at my aunt. "We need a little medical advice here. Morgan hasn't been able to sleep in over a week—"

I shot my father a dirty look. "Dad, come *on* . . ."

He put his hand on top of my head. "You can't go on like this, kiddo; you've got to get some rest."

"Do you want me to give you something to help you sleep?" my aunt asked.

"No." I started zipping and unzipping my duffel bag

again. "I just . . . I want to handle this on my own."

"Look, you've been without sleep so long you can't even think straight," my father said.

I sat back in my chair. I was starting to feel sick, that's how exhausted I was. I looked at my aunt. "Most of the stuff I'm handling. Most of the stuff I have under control."

My aunt nodded. "I'm going to call the pharmacy here and order a small prescription of sleeping pills for you, okay? We'll pick it up on our way out."

"Yeah," I said. "Okay."

She picked up the phone. "This is Dr. Hackett. I want to talk to the pharmacist, please."

My father bent down and kissed the top of my head. "I've got to run; I'll pick you up for the opening, okay?"

"Dad, wait." I followed him to the door. "Why did you do that? Why'd you have to tell her about the not sleeping thing?"

"Because, cutie, I knew *you* wouldn't." He gave me another kiss. "Get a good night's sleep, okay? See you tomorrow." I watched him walk down the hall and head for the elevators. I turned around and looked at my aunt. She was just hanging up the phone.

"I guess you think I'm crazy or something," I said.

"No," my aunt said. "I think you're tired."

"How come I can't sleep?"

"I don't know. Maybe it has something to do with stress."

"You mean Jimmy?"

"Yes."

"Maybe." I cleared my throat. "Listen, I need to tell you something . . . and I need to know if you think it's sick or weird or anything."

She put her cigarette down in the ashtray and looked at me. "What is it?"

I went over to the window and pretended to be very interested in the traffic below. "That first night at home after the accident?" I said. "I threw Jimmy's jacket away . . . but after everyone was asleep, I went down and got it out of the garbage. I wear it to bed every night. If I can't sleep and have to get up, I hide it under my mattress so Mother and Dad won't see me in it." I turned around and looked at her. "It's pretty strange, isn't it?"

"Why do you think wearing Jimmy's jacket to bed is strange?"

"I don't know. It just doesn't seem like a normal thing to do."

She tapped her cigarette against the inside of her ashtray. "I think wearing Jimmy's jacket is your way of holding on to him."

I felt heat wash over my face. "You're saying it's morbid."

"No," my aunt said firmly. "I'm saying that when you start to deal with Jimmy's death you won't feel a need to wear his jacket."

I looked away again. I had said too much and gotten myself into an area I didn't want to get into.

"Is this what it's like?" I asked. "With your patients, I mean. Is this what therapy is like?"

"Sometimes."

"Well, it hurts."

"I know," my aunt said quietly. "Sometimes it has to."

21

I *slept* that night! I slept hard, and straight through till eleven the next morning, thanks to a little red-and-white fifteen-milligram wonder of modern medicine. When I got out of bed, I pulled on my jeans and a sweater, tucked the bottle of pills into my jacket pocket, and went downstairs. I found my aunt in the entry hall; she was getting her medical bag down off the top shelf of the closet. She had a slice of pizza in her hand.

"Cold pizza for breakfast?" I asked.

"Hi, there. . . . No time for anything else; I've got an emergency. . . . Hold this for me, honey, will you?" She handed me her medical bag and her slice of pizza. She pulled her coat off a hanger. "How'd you sleep?"

I took a bite of her pizza. "Fine. I feel human again."

"You look a lot better." She leaned against the wall and pulled her boots on. "What are you going to do this afternoon? Do you want to meet me at Field's for lunch?"

"I thought I'd go over to Second City in a little

while—I want to sign up for the new semester, and if there's a workshop this afternoon, I could be a while."

"You're cutting out on me, huh?"

"You don't mind, do you?"

She smiled. "I'd never stand in the way of a future star's career; you know that." She took her medical bag and the slice of pizza from me. "You need money for a cab or anything?"

"No, I'm pretty well set."

"Okay, honey; I've got to run. I'll see you at the gallery later."

" 'Bye." I stood at the door and watched her get into the car. "Hey, the streets look icy!" I yelled. "Be careful, okay?"

My father called that afternoon, just as I was about to go out the door.

"I'm at the gallery," he said. "I thought I'd pick you and Loey up; give you a sneak preview of the show—"

"Uh, Aunt Lo's out on an emergency, and I was just about to leave for Second City to sign up for the new semester."

"And your mom's at Saks shopping for something to wear tonight! Are *all* the women in my life deserting me?!"

"Why don't you pick me up at Second City in a couple of hours, okay? You can give me a preview then, and I promise I'll be impressed."

"I'll pick you up out front. Hey, how are you feeling today?"

"Great. I actually got some sleep last night."

"So did your mom and I."

"Not funny!"

"I'll see you about quarter to five."

"Okay," I said. "Quarter to five."

Second City was pretty much deserted. I found the director of my workshop upstairs in the empty bar. He was sitting at a table reading the sports section from the *Sun-Times*.

"Hi," I said. "Where is everyone?"

"Hi, there. . . . Well, the resident company's in rehearsing and the workshop's been over for about an hour."

"It's not too late to sign up for the new semester, is it?"

"No, I don't think so; we have a few spaces left. I was getting a little worried when you didn't show up last week—I thought maybe you weren't coming back to us."

"Well, I thought . . . I thought I was going to do a play at Pheasant Run, but it didn't work out."

He nodded. "I'll go ask Joyce to make up your new membership card. Be right back."

I sat down at the table and flipped through the *Sun-Times*. I was chuckling over the comics section when this guy walked into the bar. He looked about my age, maybe a little older.

"Do you work here?" he asked.

"Me? No. I'm just a student."

"Me too. I mean, I *want* to be. I want to sign up for the workshop—"

"The workshop director'll be back in a minute."

"Thanks." He looked around. "I've never done any improvisational comedy before. My agent thinks it'll be good training for me."

"You have an agent?"

"Mostly for film work. Hey, maybe you saw a local commercial I did last September for Jewel Stores' back-to-school meat sale. I played a courteous box boy."

I smiled. "Gee, I must have missed that."

He laughed. He had a very nice laugh. Warm and friendly. "I guess I won't exactly be getting an Oscar nomination for it. How about you? What have you done professionally?"

"Nothing as glamorous as a meat commercial, I'm afraid. I studied here last semester, and I was an apprentice out at Pheasant Run for a while—"

"That's a great theater. I did *Hello, Dolly!* out there a couple of summers ago."

"You did? So did a friend of mine. Maybe you knew him. Jimmy Woolf?"

He frowned. "Jimmy Woolf . . . I'm not sure. What does he look like?"

"Tall. Tall and very lanky."

"I don't think so."

"You *must* remember him. He was one of the dancing waiters."

He shrugged. "I didn't know too many of the dancers. I was just in the chorus."

"Oh."

"Hey, you want to get a cup of coffee after we're through here? You can tell me about the workshop."

I let a brief glimmer of interest flicker before I killed it. I wasn't ready to be friends again with somebody. Not with him. Not with anyone.

"I don't think so," I said.

"There's a restaurant just down the street—"

"No, I can't. I just—I can't."

"Maybe next time, huh?"

"Yeah," I said. "Maybe."

My father was late picking me up. I kept checking my watch: fifteen minutes late. Twenty minutes. I took a couple of deep breaths of sub-zero city air. I tried to stay calm. I had warned my aunt about the icy streets, but why hadn't I warned my father? He was a good driver, but Jimmy had been a good driver too. I pulled up the collar of my jacket and watched for our car. This was like being stuck in some weird *Twilight Zone* rerun of the night Jimmy was killed. I could feel it starting all over again. I couldn't stop it: the adrenaline rush, my heart pounding wildly and out of control.

"Hey, cutie!" I heard my father yell. "Over here!" I looked across the street. My father slowed the car in mid traffic and opened the door. I ran quickly, carefully, to our car, got in, and slammed the door. My father took his foot off the brake and we started moving. "How'd it go? You get all signed up for your workshop?"

I turned to him. I couldn't keep the shakiness out of my voice. "You said *quarter to five!* Where *were* you?"

He glanced over at me, surprised. "What's wrong?"

"I don't know! When you didn't come . . . it was just like the night Jimmy was killed! I thought something had happened to you!"

"I got hung up in traffic; it's rush hour."

I put my hand on my chest. "God . . . my heart feels like it's going to explode—"

"That's anxiety," my father said. "A panic attack." He held his arm out. "Come on. Scoot over." I slid over. He put his arm around me. I couldn't stop shaking.

"You can't drive one handed," I said.

"Watch me." He zipped through the city traffic. He was a good driver, even one handed. "Listen, now— not everyone you love is going to suddenly drop out of your life like Jimmy did."

"But things happen."

"Sometimes. Not always."

I tried to take a few deep breaths and relax. I was sitting next to my father. His arm was around me. I should have felt safe, but I didn't.

"Dad . . . slow down, okay? Don't go so fast."

My father hadn't been speeding at all, but I guess he understood how scared I was, because he slowed the car down. We got some nasty horn honking from the traffic behind us, not to mention a few interesting hand gestures from the drivers who passed us. None of it seemed to faze him.

"It's going to be okay," he said. "Everything's going to be all right."

I nodded. I wanted to hear that everything would be all right. I *needed* to hear it, even if I couldn't believe it.

22

Mrs. Woolf showed up at the gallery that night. It was a shock to glance around the room and see her standing there chatting casually with my father. My mother and I looked at each other.

"You didn't know she was coming?" I asked.

"No," my mother said. "We invited her, of course. Jack too. But she wasn't sure. She hasn't gone out socially since Jimmy died."

"I should go over and say something."

"She'd like that."

"I don't know what to tell her. I don't know what to say about ditching Jimmy's funeral."

"You don't have to say anything. Enid understands."

"I don't know." I walked over to Mrs. Woolf slowly. When she saw me, her face broke into this terrific smile, and I caught a glimpse of her famous dimples. It was just automatic that we hugged.

"I'm glad you came," I whispered.

"I'm glad too."

"Is Mr. Woolf coming?"

"In a minute. He's parking the car." She held me at arms' length and looked at me. "Your mom says you're having a rough time."

This was so characteristic of Mrs. Woolf: to turn it around and worry about *me*.

"I don't know," I said. "I've had trouble sleeping and panic attacks. Outside of being a little crazy, I guess I'm fine."

Mrs. Woolf laughed. "You can't go through what we have and not end up a little crazy."

"Mrs. Woolf . . . I'm sorry about not going to the funeral. But once I got there, once I got to the church—"

"Oh, Morgan." She reached over and squeezed my hand. "You were Jimmy's friend, and you were there for him when it counted."

"I wanted to say something to you at the funeral . . . and that night at the hospital, too. I know that was a terrible time for you."

"The hardest part was the not knowing," Mrs. Woolf said. "No one at that hospital would tell me anything definite. Your aunt was the one who finally gave me a straight answer. She was in the emergency room a very short time. Something like two minutes. Then she came back out and told me Jimmy was probably not going to make it. And she asked me if I wanted to see him."

"Did you?"

"Yes," Mrs. Woolf said. "Even though I had talked to the police and the nurses, there was part of me that wouldn't believe he was in there. I had to see him . . . I wanted to say good-bye to him."

I bit my lip. Hard. I was not going to give in to a big emotional scene.

"I looked in on him for a minute, but your aunt stayed in the emergency room with him the whole time. I know it was terribly difficult for her to come out and tell me he had died."

Mrs. Woolf's eyes filled with tears. So did mine.

"Why is it," Mrs. Woolf said, "that I never seem to have a handkerchief when I need one?"

I patted my jacket pockets: no handkerchief, no Kleenex.

"Here," my mother said. She dug in her purse and handed Mrs. Woolf some Kleenex. I backed off. I was probably the one person in that room who understood exactly what Mrs. Woolf was going through, but I couldn't talk to her about it.

Mrs. Woolf blew her nose. She was smiling and crying at the same time. "I talked to your sister-in-law," she said to my mother. "She recommended a therapist out near Glen Ellyn. She says he's very nice."

"Do you have an appointment?"

"Next week."

This was really news to me. I couldn't believe it.

The gallery was packed, but I pushed my way around people until I found my aunt. She was sipping wine and talking and laughing with a bunch of her friends.

"Could I . . . I need to talk to you a minute." She stopped smiling when she saw me and followed me to a quiet corner a few feet away.

"What's wrong?" she asked.

"Mrs. Woolf said something about seeing some therapist you recommended."

"Yes," my aunt said.

"She's okay, isn't she? I mean, she's not having a nervous breakdown or anything, is she?"

"No . . . she just feels she needs a little professional help right now, that's all."

"I didn't know what to do. She started crying. I didn't know what to say."

"Fay's talking to her," my aunt said, glancing across the room. "She'll be okay."

"She must be in really bad shape if she has to go into therapy, huh?"

"No . . . I think she's coping well."

"How can you *say* that? Look at her. She's really falling apart."

"Enid's not falling apart. She's coming to terms with some of the pain she's feeling. She's handling it."

"God, I thought *I* was having problems, but at least I don't need any *professional* help—"

The minute the words were out of my mouth, I

thought about the panic attacks and not being able to sleep. I thought about the bottle of pills in my jacket pocket: They didn't just drop out of the sky. A *doctor* had prescribed them for me. I *was* getting professional help, and I hadn't even realized it.

I looked at my aunt. "I didn't want to come to you about not being able to sleep. That was Dad's idea, not mine."

"I know," my aunt said.

I stuck around that gallery for twenty more minutes; then I just had to get out of there. It was too smoky, too loud, too crowded. And everyone in that damn gallery seemed to be paired up: my mother and father, my aunt and her boyfriend, even Mr. and Mrs. Woolf. I knew they were going through a rough time, but they had each other. They held hands and walked through the gallery. They took time and really looked at the paintings.

I walked out onto Madison. I didn't go far, just a little way down the street. When I crossed the bridge over the Chicago River, I stopped and looked down into the water for a little while. A couple of years earlier Jimmy and I had stood in the same spot and watched them dye the river bright green for Saint Patrick's Day. *"Hang in there, kid,"* Jimmy had said to me that day. *"Spring is just around the corner."* Right now that green river and the promise of spring seemed a million light-years away. Right now, in the dead of winter, I stood looking down into a gray river, chunky with ice floes. I reached into my jacket pocket and took out the bottle of sleeping pills. I pitched them over the railing and watched them disappear into the water.

I didn't need the lousy pills.

I didn't need anything.

23

I wanted to handle Jimmy's death on my own, but after a couple of months I realized it was doing me in and I wasn't handling it at all. I didn't think anyone else would notice this about me, but they did. One afternoon in English:

"Can I have your quatrains, Morgan?"

"What?" I looked up into Mrs. Klein's face. "My what?"

"Last night's homework," she said. "Two quatrains—you forgot to turn them in at the beginning of the period."

"Oh," I said. I couldn't even remember what a quatrain *was*, let alone having been assigned to write one. "I don't exactly have my homework, Mrs. Klein."

"Where is it?"

Jody shot me a look that said: "Make something up!" And who knows? In the old days I probably would have thought fast and had an ironclad excuse ready for Mrs. Klein. But not this time. This time I just couldn't think. This time I just didn't care.

"I guess I forgot to do it," I said.

"Stay after when the bell rings. I want to talk to you."

As soon as Mrs. Klein had gone back up to her desk, Jody leaned over and whispered, "You're a lot braver than I am, Morgan. She's been talking about those damn quatrains for over a week now."

"She has? I guess I haven't been paying attention. . . ."

"Hey, are you okay? You've seemed kind of . . . I don't know . . . out of it lately. I see you in the halls, I say hi to you, and you act like you don't even hear me."

"No, I *hear* you. I just . . ." I couldn't look at her. I stared straight ahead. My eyes stung, and everything written on the blackboard blurred in a chalky mess. I didn't know *what* was wrong with me exactly.

After the bell had rung, after everyone had filed out, Jody stood up and said quietly: "I don't think anyone should have to face Mrs. Klein alone—want me to stick around?"

"Oh . . . Jody, thanks, but I'm okay."

"You always do that," she said.

"What?"

"You always say you're okay, even when you're not."

Jimmy had said that to me once, and it was okay

166

for him to say it because he was Jimmy, but that didn't give Jody or anyone else the right to say it.

I looked at Jody. "I said I'm *okay*. You better get going or you'll be late for your next class."

Jody shrugged and picked up her books and walked out. I just sat there and watched her go. I didn't say anything to stop her, even though part of me wanted her to stay.

"Morgan?" Mrs. Klein said. "Come on up here, won't you? I don't have a class this period, and we can talk."

I picked up my books and went up to one of the desks at the front of the room. I sat down. Mrs. Klein opened her grade book and turned it around so I could see it. She ran her finger along a line of D's and F's.

"Your grades have really started slipping lately," she said. "There's a lot of work you haven't turned in."

"Oh," I said.

"And you seem to be having a lot of trouble concentrating in class."

"If it's about the quatrains . . . I'll do them tonight and hand them in first thing tomorrow."

"No, it's not just that. . . . I called your mother this morning and asked her to come in for a conference."

"What? *Why*?"

"I know you're going through a difficult time right now, but—"

"What did my mother tell you?"

167

"But I want you to understand that you're probably facing an incomplete on your report card this quarter."

"What exactly did my mother tell you?"

"She reminded me about your friend . . . about his death."

I picked up my books.

"You know, an incomplete isn't the end of the world. You can make up the work next quarter or even in summer school—"

I stood up. "I'll get the work turned in. All of it. I'll get it turned in."

"If I can do anything," Mrs. Klein said. "Help you get caught up after school—"

"No, I don't need any help."

"I just want you to know I understand—"

"You don't," I said. "No one does."

I turned around and walked out. I went to my locker, dumped my books in, and pulled out my jacket and boots. I walked past three hall monitors and right out of the building. It was a little trick I had learned from Jimmy: Act like you know what you're doing and where you're going, and no one will bother you.

I ended up spending seventh period down at the boathouse by Lake Ellyn. I stood just inside the door and watched a couple of little kids lacing up their skates out on the pier. They got out on the ice, and even though one of them was just a beginner, they were both doing a pretty good job. Jimmy had tried to teach

168

me to skate once, but I was just no good at it. Now I was sorry I hadn't tried harder. Watching those kids go around and around on the ice made me feel bad. I bit my thumbnail and watched them for the longest time.

In a way I felt sorry for those kids: They were having the time of their life, and they didn't even know it.

24

"I just got a call from the school," my mother said as soon as I walked in the door. "They said you didn't show up for seventh period."

"Mrs. Klein says she talked to you."

"Yeah, this morning."

"I guess it looks like I'm failing English. . . ."

"I don't care about the damn English work," my mother said. "I only care about *you*, about what's *happening* to you."

"I don't know," I said. I looked at her. "I don't even know."

"That night Jimmy was killed," my mother said, "it hit you so hard . . . so *hard* . . . there was absolutely no color in your face, no expression—"

"I don't want to talk about that night," I said.

"I was worried about you because you weren't even talking coherently—and before Loey gave you that shot she said . . . she said the whole thing hadn't caught up with you yet. Do you remember that?"

"Yeah. Yeah, I remember."

"I think maybe it's finally catching up with you now, don't you think?"

I was a bunch of knots inside. "I guess. I don't know." I started up the stairs. "Can we talk about this later? I'm just very tired." I went up to my bedroom, yanked off my boots, and collapsed on the bed. This overwhelming fatigue was swallowing me up. I just wanted to be left alone and not have to talk to or see anyone, but in a couple of minutes I noticed my mother standing in the doorway.

"We haven't talked about this before," she said. "But . . . you know, Enid's feeling a lot better since she started seeing that doctor Loey recommended—"

"I'm not seeing any therapist."

"Enid says he's easy to talk to. Why don't you let me call and make an appointment for you."

"No! I'm glad it's working out for Mrs. Woolf. I'm glad she's feeling better. But I couldn't ever do it. Talk to someone about Jimmy. I couldn't. It's too private."

My mother ran her fingers through her hair. "I think maybe you pushed it—going back to school and everything so soon after Jimmy's death."

"Maybe . . ."

She nodded. "Try to get some rest." She started out the door, then she turned around and looked at me. "Where did you go when you were supposed to be in seventh period? What did you do?"

"I went down to the lake—I stood in the boathouse and watched the ice skaters."

"Oh, Morgan, it's so cold down there! Honestly, the thought of you all alone down at that boathouse—"

"I didn't know what else to do."

"You could have called *me!*"

"I didn't think. I wasn't sure you'd understand."

My mother looked at me. She seemed hurt. "You know, I wish you'd tell me some of the things going on in your life. I do understand. . . ."

"I want to tell you stuff, I really do. Look, can't we talk about this later? I'm just very tired. I had a crummy day and I'm just very tired."

"I hope you get some rest. We'll talk later, okay?"

"Yeah," I said. "Okay."

We would not talk later or anytime else. I had my own system of working things out, my own way of facing things and not facing them. These methods did not include having a heart-to-heart chat with my mother. I couldn't let her in. I just couldn't. I wasn't letting *anyone* get close to me again. Too dangerous. I couldn't share the bad stuff I was feeling with anyone. Jimmy was the one I could have talked to. Jimmy was the one who would have understood. But Jimmy wasn't here now, and I had to handle the sadness alone. Only instead of handling it, I put it on hold. To be dealt with later.

This was my detour system.

∽ 25 ∾

My parents let me lie around in bed for exactly three weeks. Then one morning my father came into my bedroom and pulled the sheet down to my nose.

"I don't think it's such a hot idea, little one, your staying in bed all the time like this."

"I just need to be by myself for a little while," I said. "I need some time alone to figure things out."

He sat down on the bed and looked at me. "Just exactly how bad are you feeling? Tell me."

I peeked at him over the sheet. "What do you mean?"

"Well, I guess I'm asking you if you're so unhappy you're thinking of hurting yourself. I guess I'm asking you if you're thinking of suicide."

"*What?*" That really got my attention. "Am I thinking about *what?*"

"Are you thinking about hurting yourself?"

"No!" I yanked the sheet down to my chin. "I'm not like that! I'm very . . . stable! I'm not a self-destructor!"

"I know you're not," my father said quietly. "And I

know you're stable. But sometimes even very stable people get depressed, and that's what I'm talking about here, kiddo. Depression."

I couldn't believe my father was sitting there talking to me about suicide the way most fathers might ask their daughters how they want their hamburger done at a barbecue.

"I'll handle this," I said. "I'll handle what I'm going through and I'll be okay."

"Now you're telling me what you think I want to hear. I want to know how you *really* feel."

"You want to know how I *really* feel? I feel dead inside, okay?! I wish *I* had been killed that night instead of Jimmy!" There. I had said it.

"Why?" my father asked softly. "Why do you wish you had been killed?"

"I don't know! Because Jimmy could have made it without me, but I can't make it without him!"

"Yes, you can."

"But I don't *want* to!" My father and I looked at each other. There was just this awful silence. I looked away, then I felt his hand on mine.

"When you were little, it was easy," my father said. "You thought I could fix anything—"

"No one can fix this," I said.

"No."

"I'm scared," I said. "It scares me to feel this way."

"I know," my father said. "Tell you what—why don't we get you out of the house for a little while,

174

okay? Let's go for a short walk. Maybe just down to the corner and back."

"A walk? Did I hear you right? A *walk*?"

"Depression's a funny thing," my father said. "The more you lie around, the more depressed you get."

"Dad, come on—going for a walk isn't going to change anything."

"Yes, it will," he said. "It'll make your father happy to see you in a vertical position for a change."

"I don't know. I feel kind of shaky about going out."

"I'll be right there; nothing's going to happen."

I looked at him. "Do you think I'm crazy?"

"A little," my father said, and I laughed. For the first time in weeks. It felt terrific.

My father smiled. "Wait for you outside."

I got dressed and went downstairs. My father was waiting for me out on the sidewalk in front of our house. When he saw me, he smiled and held out his hand.

"It's a beautiful day, isn't it?"

"Yeah," I said. I took his hand and we started walking. The sun was very strong; ice patches were slowly melting into warm puddles. The whole season had started changing while I was up in my room hibernating.

"I've never had a close friend die," my father said, "so I can't pretend to know what you're going through—"

"I can't figure all this stuff out! It's like it's all tangled

175

up! It started after Jimmy was killed. I *know* that. But knowing doesn't make it any easier to untangle."

"You'll get it untangled."

"I got through Jimmy's *death* okay, but what I can't figure out is how to get through my *life* without him."

"Like the Novocain's finally wearing off and you're beginning to feel a little pain?"

"Yeah . . ." We hit the corner, turned around, and started walking back. I was wearing tennis shoes, and they were soaked from all the slush we'd been walking through. "You know, I never cried once after he was killed," I said. "I don't know why, but I never did." I looked at my father. "Do you think that's wrong?"

"No . . . I think everybody probably handles something like this in their own way. Look at Enid. She did enough crying for both of you."

I smiled. "Yeah." A sudden memory flash: Jimmy, whirling me around and around his porch one hot summer day. I wanted to blot it out. I tried to. I couldn't. "God, I'm remembering stuff about him and I don't *want* to!"

"Come here," my father said. He put his arm around me and pulled me into a hug. It was nice. Safe. I felt anchored to someone again. We walked home like that. On the way into the house I noticed something I hadn't seen before: tulips, peeking up around the big tree out front.

Spring was definitely on the way.

26

The next morning I decided to take the plunge and go back to school. When I told my mother at breakfast, she practically chased me around the table with a box of cornflakes.

"No!" I said. "I'm not hungry!"

"You're going back to school, you've got to have something to eat—"

"If I have anything more than coffee, I'll throw up."

"Oh," my mother said. "Oh. All right, then. Just coffee."

"You have to write me a note. Just keep it simple. Something like 'Please excuse Morgan's absence from school, but she went nuts for a while. Although she may foam at the mouth from time to time, she poses no serious threats to students or teachers.' "

"Honestly," my mother said. She set a mug down in front of me and filled it with coffee. "You okay about going back? How do you feel about it?"

"I'm more or less petrified."

"Are you? Do you realize you've never done that

177

before? Told me how you felt, straight out like that?"

"Ta da," I said. I traced the rim of my coffee cup with one finger. "No, what I mean is . . . I never meant to keep anything from you. I'm just not too great about talking about what's inside. But I guess you know that."

"It's a family characteristic," my mother said. "All on the Hackett side, I might add. You get it right from your father. And your aunt. Your father says she was just like you when she was your age."

"Really?" I took a sip of coffee. I tried to picture my aunt at seventeen, walking around hunched over her science books, quiet like me and alone like me. It was a picture I couldn't quite get out of my head. "What was it like for you when *you* were in high school?" I asked. "Did you have a lot of friends?"

"Well, Enid and I were friends, of course," my mother said. She poured herself a cup of coffee and sat down. "But we sort of went our separate ways after high school."

"I wonder if that would have happened to Jimmy and me after we graduated," I said. "I wonder if we would have drifted apart."

"Jimmy thought you were pretty special, you know. I don't think there's any way he would have just let you drift away from him."

"I hope not. I hope we would have stayed close."

* * *

Jody cornered me in the cafeteria. I was sitting alone at a table trying to peel the Saran Wrap off a peanut butter and jelly sandwich when suddenly there she was—she dumped her books and sack lunch on the table and sat down next to me.

"Welcome back," she said. "What was wrong with you, anyway?"

"Hi. It's a long story."

"You must really have been sick. You were gone over a month, weren't you?"

"I wasn't sick, Jody. Jimmy's death finally caught up with me and I really started having problems. I guess I sort of cracked up."

Jody didn't say anything. She turned her brown paper bag upside down. A sandwich, a couple of cookies fell out. An apple rolled across the table, and I stopped it with my hand. "Tuna fish again," she said. She looked at me. "I didn't know things were that bad for you."

"Neither did I. You know something, Jody? Three weeks from Sunday I'm going to be eighteen, but inside . . . inside I feel like I'm a little kid trying to cut it in a great big world."

"I feel that way sometimes too. I think it's nature's way of letting us know what life as an adult is going to be like. Sort of like a preview of coming attractions."

"Maybe." I took a bite out of my sandwich. "What happened in English while I was gone? Did I miss a lot?"

179

"She's been cramming a lot of Robert Frost down our throats. We have to turn in a paper Wednesday analyzing 'The Road Not Taken,' and we have to memorize the first twenty lines of 'Birches' by Friday—"

"God, there's just no way I'll be able to make everything up by the end of the quarter."

"Sure you will, Morgan. You can do anything."

"Thanks, but I don't know . . . just making myself get out of bed and come to school was a major accomplishment for me. I'm not sure I'll be able to graduate on time. I might have to go to summer school."

"I guess this has been a pretty bad time for you."

"Yeah."

"How are you now? Are you okay?"

"No," I said. "But let's keep it our little secret, okay?"

Jody smiled. "Trade you half a tuna fish for half of your peanut butter and jelly."

"Jody," I said, "I *hate* tuna fish."

She picked up half of my sandwich and took a big bite out of it. "Who doesn't?" she said.

27

Jimmy's birthday was April twentieth, four days before mine. I hadn't gone to his funeral, but I figured the least I could do was to celebrate his birth. I stopped by Kar-Lee's after school, bought a half dozen roses, and took them to his mother. Taking flowers to his mother made a lot more sense to me than taking them to his grave, but I was nervous about it. I wasn't sure how Mrs. Woolf would take it. After I pulled into the Woolfs' driveway, it took me a good five minutes to get out of the car. The porch looked so quiet, so different, so dead compared to the last time I'd stood on it, the day Jimmy had whirled me around and around because he was so happy he'd gotten the callback at his audition. I was sitting in the car memory tripping when the kitchen window opened. Mrs. Woolf leaned her elbows out on the sill and looked at me.

"Are you going to sit out there in that car all day, Morgan Hackett, or are you going to come in and say hello?"

"Hi," I said.

"Hi yourself. Come on back to the kitchen; I'm making coffee."

It was weird being back in Jimmy's house. I had practically grown up in this house; it was my second home, but now I felt out of place. Like I didn't belong.

"Be careful on the hall floor," Mrs. Woolf hollered from the kitchen. "I just waxed it; it might be slippery."

I had the feeling I had interrupted Mrs. Woolf's spring cleaning. The living-room furniture had been pushed back against one wall, the rug rolled up, the floor waxed. There were some cardboard boxes at the foot of the stairs, but I didn't think too much of them at the time. I tiptoed down the hall and into the kitchen.

"Did I come at a bad time?" I asked.

She looked up from the coffeepot. "You? Never. Come on in and sit down."

"I didn't forget," I said. I handed her the flowers. "I've been thinking about him all day. It's hard for me, because we always celebrated our birthdays together."

"I know," Mrs. Woolf said. "These are beautiful, Morgan. Thank you." She took a large glass pitcher out of the dish drain, filled it with water, and put the flowers in it. "You know, I've been thinking a lot about you today too. How've you been doing?"

"Some days are easier than other days," I said. "Jimmy spoiled me, you know. No one else measures up."

"He thought an awful lot of you, too, Morgan. You know that, don't you?"

"I think so. I know he did."

"Jimmy talked about wanting to do something special for your eighteenth birthday. I don't know what he had in mind, but I went ahead and did something anyway. Wait here a second."

I poured the coffee while she was gone. Being with Mrs. Woolf without Jimmy was like being in a puzzle with one of the pieces missing. I think in the back of my head I was waiting for someone to come along and put in the missing piece, someone to make things all right again.

Mrs. Woolf came back and handed me a small battered box. I took the lid off; inside was a tiny gold ring with a J engraved on it.

"It was Jimmy's baby ring," Mrs. Woolf said. "I had it made a little bigger so you could wear it."

"Are you sure you want to give this to me?" I asked. I slipped it on my little finger. A perfect fit. "Don't you want to keep it?"

"What I *want*," Mrs. Woolf said, taking my hand, "is for you to have something of Jimmy's." When she said it like that, I started to feel pretty good. Warm. Like I'd had a nice shot of brandy.

"This really means a lot to me. Thanks."

"Happy eighteen, Morgan." She sat down and took a sip of coffee. "Jack and I are doing something for Jimmy, too. For his birthday. We're establishing a scholarship at his dance school."

"He'd like that," I said. I thought it was a nice idea,

giving someone else a shot at the career Jimmy couldn't have.

"You know, Morgan . . . I have something to tell you, and I'm not exactly sure how to go about it."

The warm glow receded. I didn't want to hear bad news. I was no longer good at coping with bad news. I had had enough bad news to last me a lifetime, but I braced myself for it anyway.

"What is it?" I asked.

"Jack has accepted a transfer . . . to Kansas City . . . and we'll be moving as soon as we can sell the house."

"*Moving*," I said. "No . . ."

"I know I should have mentioned it earlier, but it just wasn't definite until today."

"Mrs. Woolf, *why*? Is it because of what happened? Is it because of Jimmy?"

"No. Jack was offered this promotion last fall, but we didn't want Jimmy to have to change schools his senior year. It's really all right, Morgan. We're in pretty good shape. We're looking forward to this move; we're not running away from anything."

It just didn't seem fair. Jimmy, then the Woolfs. Too much was changing and too fast.

"Have you told Mother yet?" I asked.

"No. Not yet."

"She's not going to like it," I said. "She's really going to miss you. So am I."

Mrs. Woolf smiled. "You're my second kid, you

know, and I'm not too crazy about being away from *you* either."

"Is that why you're doing all this cleaning? Because of the move? Is there anything I can help with? Anything I can do?"

"Yes," Mrs. Woolf said. "You can come over here and give me a hug."

I got up and went over and hugged her. After a minute I said, "Is it really okay? Are you happy about the move, I mean?"

"Yes. Really."

"That's all that matters, then."

It really rattled me, the idea of Mr. and Mrs. Woolf moving. But why? It wasn't like they could take Jimmy away from me, because he was already gone, so what exactly was wrong? It was almost like I couldn't accept it. It was funny how my mind kept trying to adjust the picture and make it right, when it wasn't the picture that needed adjusting, it was me.

⟨ 28 ⟩

Jody was waiting for me by my locker Friday afternoon after fourth period.

"Sunday's your birthday, isn't it?" she said. "Here." She pushed a huge paper bag at me.

"How'd you know my birthday's Sunday?"

"You mentioned it that day you came back to school, remember?"

I opened the bag and took out a floppy-brimmed straw hat.

"Are you kidding?" I said. I put the hat on my head. The brim was so big it touched my shoulders. "Jody— don't get me wrong—I mean, it's lovely and all that, but you don't expect me to wear this around school, do you?"

"Of course not. I expect you to wear it when we *ditch* school."

"Ditch? Oh, no . . ."

"I have the afternoon all planned, Morgan. We'll get some hamburgers or something at Prince Castle and eat them down by the lake—"

"I am not *ditching*! I missed enough school when I was . . . you know, I cracked up for a while and I missed a lot of school."

"That doesn't count. Missing school because you're cracking up is understandable. It's *excusable*. I'm talking about out-and-out ditching. Ditching just to have fun."

"No, thanks."

"Come on. Didn't you ever do anything crazy on the spur of the moment?"

I had to think about that. When Jimmy was around I did a lot of crazy and unplanned things. It had been a long time. Too long, maybe.

"All right," I said.

"Well, come on then! Dump your books in your locker and let's get out of here before some pervert of a hall monitor tries to stop us."

I opened my locker and threw my books in it. "What happens?" I said. "I mean, the attendance office'll find out about it, won't they?"

"A couple hours' detention. Big deal. You'll love it. It's like a party."

"Okay, Jody, okay," I said. "But this better be one hell of an afternoon if I'm going to have to pay for it by spending some Saturday morning in detention hall."

We got a sack of hamburgers and French fries at Prince Castle and walked down to the park by Lake Ellyn.

"Let's sit on the swings and eat," Jody said. "Wait a second. Here." She took one of the hamburgers out of the sack and unwrapped it. She handed it to me. "Hold that for a second. We have to do this properly." She unhooked her backpack from her shoulder and unzipped it. She rummaged around in the bottom of it and took out a pink candle and a pack of matches.

"I don't believe this," I said.

"Believe it. This is an official birthday hamburger." She stuck the candle in the hamburger and lit it. "Make a wish," she said.

I shut my eyes and blew out the candle. I didn't make a wish; wishing for something I couldn't have seemed like a big waste of time.

"Don't tell me what you wished for," she said. "If you tell, it won't come true." She sat down on the swing next to me and started in on her French fries. "Did I tell you I'm not going to Northwestern? They don't want me. Neither does the University of Wisconsin, where my boyfriend goes. I got both rejections on the same day, can you believe that?"

"Where are you going to go, then?"

"I don't know. College of DuPage, maybe. It'd save a lot of money."

"I sort of envy you," I said. "At least you know you want to go to college. I'm not sure *what* I want to do."

"I thought you were going to be an actress."

"So did I. Now I'm not so sure. It's like my wanting

to do it was all tied up with Jimmy or something. I just don't know if it's important anymore."

"So what are you going to do?"

"I wish I knew."

"You should stick with it, Morgan. The theater, I mean. You'll be mad someday if you don't."

"Yeah," I said smiling. "Maybe you're right."

We were rolling around like that when it occurred to me that maybe a wish had been answered after all, that maybe I had a friend. Not a friend like Jimmy, maybe, but a friend anyway. It was nice.

"Here," Jody said. "Give me your garbage." She held out the paper bag, and I stuffed our empty French fry and hamburger wrappers into it. She took it over to a green metal trash can and tossed it in. "Let's see who can get highest on the swings," she said. "We'll make it like a contest, okay?"

"Are you crazy?"

"Yes, I'm crazy and so are you. Come on. You're going to be eighteen Sunday. An adult. Who knows when you'll get another chance to be in a contest like this?"

"Okay, Jody, all right, as long as you put it that way . . ."

Side by side we swung, like little kids do, our legs pumping. My hat flew off and sailed to the ground like a straw Frisbee. We got so high on those swings, I had to hang on for dear life.

189

"Hey, Jody!" I yelled. "This has really been a great afternoon!"

"Yeah?" she hollered back. "Worth the detention?"

"Absolutely!"

"I'm glad you feel that way, Morgan! Guess who's in charge of detention this month?"

"Who?"

"Mrs. Klein, that's who!"

I started laughing. I was getting back to my old self, where I could laugh easily. "Hey, Jody, guess what! Mrs. Klein's okay! She tried to help me when I was having problems! She's okay! She really is!"

Jody looked at me wide-eyed. "You're not only crazy," she yelled, "you're senile!"

"Hey, what do you expect? I'm almost eighteen, remember?"

I just couldn't stop laughing. It was strange and wonderful, rediscovering the power of uncontrolled laughter. I pumped the swing as hard as I could. I threw my head back. I felt like maybe I could touch the trees. Inside I was ten years old again. I felt silly. Giddy.

Free.

29

I wanted to do something for Jimmy, something private, something no one else knew about. Something that was just between him and me. I went down to the DuPage Trust and closed out my savings account. It wasn't a lot of money, less than two hundred dollars, but it was enough to make a nice contribution to the scholarship fund at Jimmy's dance school, which was what I'd decided to do.

"I'm going into the city today," I told my mother Saturday morning. "You know. Knock around. Go to Field's. Do some shopping."

"Do you need any money?"

"No, I'm okay," I said. "I'll be back around five."

"That jacket isn't going to be enough," my mother said. "You better take your coat and an umbrella; it's supposed to rain—"

"Are you kidding? There isn't a cloud in the sky!"

Mothers are always right. I got caught while I was crossing the bridge over the Chicago River, and believe me, I got caught good. The rain came fast and furious. Cabs got snatched up. People stopped ambling and started bustling. Me too. I ran the few blocks to Jimmy's dance school, pulled open the glass double doors, and collapsed against the wall. I tried to catch my breath and shake off some of the wetness.

"You picked a hell of a day to go out without a raincoat," I heard someone say. "Didn't you hear the weather report?"

"Only from my mother," I said. The person I was talking to was a young woman. A dancer, I was sure, because she was built tall and lean like Robin-the-toothpick and walked with the same kind of athletic grace.

"Here," she said. "Catch." She took the towel that was draped around her neck and tossed it to me.

"Thanks." I started drying myself off. "Listen, maybe you can help me—I guess I'm looking for the registrar or someone who handles tuition."

"Most everyone's out to lunch now. Did you want to sign up for classes?"

"No. I was a friend of Jimmy Woolf's, and I want to make a contribution to his scholarship fund."

"The scholarship's closed," the girl said. "They made the decision yesterday."

"Oh," I said. I was really disappointed. "Who got it? Who did they give it to?"

"One of the first-year students. Jimmy worked with

him a lot; taught him all of the old movie stuff. The Fred Astaire stuff."

"Well," I said, nodding, "I'm glad they gave it to someone who's interested in the same kind of dancing Jimmy was."

"It was a nice thing for his parents to do. The scholarship, I mean. The boy who got it was going to have to drop out because he couldn't afford the tuition."

"I'm glad they gave it to someone who knew Jimmy."

"You were a friend of Jimmy's?"

"Yes," I said.

"Everyone around here was really devastated when we heard about it—about what happened—"

I started getting uncomfortable. "Yeah, I know."

"Hey, would you . . . do you want to meet the boy who won the scholarship? I think he's rehearsing down the hall in one of the practice rooms."

"Oh," I said. "No . . . no, I really have to be going." I folded the towel and handed it back to her. "If I leave right now, I think I can probably catch the next train home."

"I have to get going too. I have an audition at three, and I want to rehearse for it. It was nice talking to someone who knew Jimmy—I wish we could have talked longer."

"Thanks. So do I."

" 'Bye."

"Yeah, 'bye." I watched her run up a flight of stairs.

I turned around, pulled my collar up, pushed open the glass doors. I felt like the whole afternoon had been one huge wet waste of time. I was halfway out into the rain when I heard it: a song coming from one of the practice rooms. A song from the movie *Swing Time*. A song Jimmy and I had danced to a million times, the summer we were ten. The summer he discovered Fred Astaire and fell in love with dancing. The recording sounded old—the scratches were louder than the music; still, you could hear Fred Astaire, just barely:

> *Nothing's impossible I have found,*
> *for when my chin is on the ground,*
> *I pick myself up,*
> *dust myself off,*
> *start all over again.*

I came back inside and walked slowly down the hall toward the music. I peeked inside the practice room. It was a beautiful room: neat brown-brick walls, huge windows that faced skyscrapers and gave a spectacular view of the storm, a well-worn wooden floor, and those mirrors! Ceiling to floor, parallel to the windows, along the whole length of the room. I stood just inside the door and watched the boy who had won Jimmy's scholarship. He was a young boy, maybe about fourteen, and he was totally wrapped up in his dancing, very serious about it. He was good. He was very good. Loose and relaxed and self-assured, just like Jimmy. I could see in his dance the signature of Jimmy's style. It was like this kid was signing his name with Jimmy's handwriting. It bothered me, sort of.

"Hi," the kid said, whirling by me. He stopped dancing and put his hands on his knees and tried to catch his breath. "I'm having a little trouble with the turns. . . ."

"No, it looks good. Do you . . . you don't mind if I watch, do you? This is one of my favorite routines."

"I like an audience," the boy said. He did some bending and stretching, the same loosening-up exercises I'd seen Jimmy do hundreds of times. "Are you a dancer?" he asked.

I shook my head. "Just a Fred Astaire fan."

"Me too. I love this song. It's classic Astaire, don't you think?"

"Yeah. . . . I haven't heard this song since I was about ten—a friend and I spent the entire summer doing the dances from *Swing Time*, only I think he made a much better Fred Astaire than I did a Ginger Rogers."

"*Swing Time*'s my all-time favorite movie," the boy said. He tilted his head to the side and listened to the music, like he was waiting for just the right place to start dancing again. "Here comes the chorus," he said, holding out his hand in a matter-of-fact way. "Remember this part? Want to give it a try?"

I just automatically took his hand. He put his arm around my back. It felt good. Sometimes I think that was what I missed most about Jimmy: good old-fashioned body heat. The boy started whirling me around and around the room. I shut my eyes. Partly because I was dizzy, mostly because I wanted to be back in Jimmy's arms again, even if it was only a big fake.

> *Don't lose your confidence if you slip,*
> *be grateful for a pleasant trip,*
> *And pick yourself up,*
> *dust yourself off,*
> *start all over again.*

I could almost pretend I was safe again. I could almost pretend Jimmy was whirling me around and around his front porch like he used to. I could almost pretend he had never been killed. Almost. But not quite.

"I have to go," I said suddenly. I pushed away from the boy and headed for the door.

"Hey, what's wrong?" he asked.

"Nothing. I just have to go." I ran down the hall. I banged into a couple dancers coming back from lunch, but I just kept on going.

It is not natural, I thought, *for seventeen-year-olds to get killed. It is not normal. It is not the way things were meant to be.*

Never mind the rain. Never mind the wind. The important thing was to stay calm and not give in, not give in to the panic. After I had walked a couple of blocks, my heart started pounding. Another block and I was unable to breathe. My hands started shaking. I ducked into an office building and called my aunt from a pay phone in the lobby. I had to go through her damn answering service. I finally reached her at some restaurant.

"I thought I had everything worked out," I said. It was hard for me to talk; my throat muscles felt paralyzed. "I don't know what's happening to me; I need to see you."

"Where are you?" my aunt asked. "Are you in the city?"

"I'm in some office building on Wacker. I have to see you."

"I'll meet you at the hospital. Can you make it over there?"

"Yes."

"I'm leaving right now, and I want you to do the same thing, okay?"

"Okay," I said.

What it boiled down to was this: I was alone, truly alone. There wasn't anyone, anywhere, who could take Jimmy's place. Maybe the school could replace him with another dancer, but what was *I* supposed to do?

The world could go on very nicely without him, maybe, but *I* couldn't. No matter how many new people I met, no matter how many new friends I made, I wouldn't ever have the same kind of relationship I'd had with Jimmy. That part of my life was gone forever. Why had it taken me so long to figure this out?

Why had I been so dumb?

30

By the time I got to the hospital, I was shaking so hard people turned and looked at me. The harder I tried not to shake, the worse it got. I took the elevator up to the psych floor. When I got off, I walked right past the nurses' station without bothering to check in with anyone. I walked down the hall to my aunt's office. I tried the door. It was locked.

"She's on her way, Morgan."

I turned around. Mrs. Getz was standing there.

"I talked to her a few minutes ago," Mrs. Getz said. "She asked me to look after you until she got here—"

"I don't need looking after. I don't. I'll just sit over here and wait for her." I walked a little way down the hall and sat on an upholstered bench. I couldn't stop shaking, so I tried to hide it by jamming my fists down into my jacket pockets. It was the exact same thing I'd done the night Jimmy was killed.

"Are you going to be okay until she gets here?" Mrs. Getz asked. "Why don't you let me have one of the other doctors take a look at you?"

"No, I want my aunt. I just want to wait here for my aunt."

"All right, Morgan, it's okay. I'll be at the nurses' station if you want anything. Try to hang on; I'm sure she'll be here in a few minutes."

It was at least fifteen more minutes before my aunt came. I was sitting there hunched over my toes when I heard her say quietly to Mrs. Getz: "How's she doing, Betty?"

"Not too good," Mrs. Getz said. "She's over there."

I looked up. I was torn between wanting my aunt's help and not wanting her to see me like this. She walked over and put her hand on my face. There was no smile. Her eyes were penetrating. "Hello, love . . . what's the trouble?"

I wanted to explain things to her. I tried to. I couldn't.

"I know you're uncomfortable, honey—can you talk?"

"I need something," I whispered. "A tranquilizer or something. I don't feel very good."

My aunt didn't say anything. She sat down beside me and unzipped my jacket. "Let's get you out of this; it's soaking wet. Betty?" She looked over her shoulder at Mrs. Getz. "Get me a blanket, will you?"

"You'll give me something, won't you? A tranquilizer or something? I can't stand feeling this way—"

"I want you to try to slow your breathing down."

"I *can't*."

"*Try*."

I just sat there while she tugged off my jacket. She grasped my wrist and looked at her watch. It occurred to me that maybe she had no intention of giving me anything, that maybe she had missed the point.

"My *heart's* racing—"

"It sure is," my aunt said. Mrs. Getz came over and put a heavy blanket across my shoulders, and I clutched the edges of it tight against me.

"Let's go into my office," my aunt said quietly. She folded up my wet jacket and went over and unlocked the door to her office. "Come on," she said. "I want to talk to you." I stood up slowly and followed her. My legs felt funny. Weak. Like I hadn't used them in a long time.

As soon as we were in her office, as soon as she shut the door, I said, "I really think I need something. Something like a tranquilizer."

"I don't want to give you any tranquilizers, honey," my aunt said. "Why don't you sit down, okay? I want to get some of these lights on. . . ."

I sat down on the couch. I couldn't believe how calmly she was acting. Here I was, cracking up, and she was walking around the office, turning on lights, hanging up my jacket, taking off her raincoat.

"You gave me something the night Jimmy was killed," I said. "You gave me a shot that night, remember?"

"That was different."

"I can't stand feeling this way. I really think I'm starting to lose it."

"Lose what?"

"I'm afraid I'm going crazy."

My aunt came over and sat down on the coffee table facing the couch. She pushed her sweater sleeves up to her elbows. "You're not afraid of going crazy. You're afraid of losing control."

"I don't like not being in control."

"I know you don't. Tell me what happened. What kicked all this off, hmm?"

"I went by Jimmy's dance school. I wanted to—I was going to make a contribution to his scholarship fund."

"Why do you think that set off an anxiety attack?"

I pulled the blanket tight around me. I wanted to hide inside it. "This isn't an anxiety attack. It's more than that. It's like a breakdown or something."

"I don't think you're having a breakdown," my aunt said gently. "What exactly happened at Jimmy's dance school?"

I looked at her. "I guess I'm afraid if I start talking about it, I'll fall apart."

"Would it really be so terrible if you lost control a little? What would happen if you gave in to what you're feeling?"

"I don't *know*. Maybe it would push me right over the edge."

"Maybe it would help you start healing."

"Maybe it would hurt."

My aunt nodded. "All the times I gave you shots,

took out splinters, patched you up? I always told you when it was going to hurt, didn't I?"

"Yes," I said.

"This is going to hurt too. Before you can start to heal, you'll have to let Jimmy go. And it's going to hurt."

I let out a shaky breath. I was going to cry, no two ways about it. I could feel the tears collect in my eyes and start to spill down my face. "I went by the school," I said. I wiped my face with the back of my hand. "I went by the school and I met the kid who's taking Jimmy's place."

"What do you mean, 'taking Jimmy's place'?" my aunt asked softly. "Are those his words or yours?"

"Jimmy and I had something, something special, and I just realized this afternoon that I'll never have that with someone again."

"Maybe not the exact same thing, no."

"Nobody understands me like he did, and it's like I'm all alone now."

My aunt smiled. She took my hand. "Well. Not entirely alone."

"It never would have happened if I hadn't been along that night. He only took North Wells because he had to drop me off."

"The only person who should feel any guilt over Jimmy's death is that bastard who killed him, do you understand? You don't know *what* street Jimmy would have taken if he'd been alone that night. No one does."

I could see myself waiting on North Wells that night. Watching the street and waiting for Jimmy. Jimmy, who never came.

"My heart," I whispered. "I can feel my *heart*."

"Your heart is very strong," my aunt said.

"Please just give me something."

"No." She leaned forward and looked at me. "You can handle this. Just let it come, honey."

I could feel all the sadness I'd kept locked inside me rise and catch in my throat. I could *feel* it coming: everything I'd avoided, pushed away, wouldn't look at. I knew it was going to hit. My aunt must have known too, because she moved over onto the couch and put her arms around me. I buried my face in her sweater and cried. I was crying for Jimmy and all that he meant to me, for our shattered friendship, for those two ten-year-olds who were once again whirling around and around a porch one hot summer day, those two kids who had the world and didn't even know it. I hung on to my aunt's sweater and cried until I was all cried out, until my head hurt and my eyes were swollen, until I was bone tired. No one told me letting go of someone you love is just damn hard work.

"It's not fair," I said. My voice was hoarse, and all my insides felt like they had been scraped raw. "He was an artist and he would have touched a lot of people's lives."

"He touched *your* life," my aunt said. "And the people you meet will know Jimmy through you . . .

because you'll touch *their* lives." She leaned over and grabbed a box of Kleenex off the coffee table and handed it to me. I pulled out sheet after sheet and wiped my eyes and nose. My head was hot and swimming.

"That kid at the dance school," I said. "It's like he stole everything Jimmy taught him and now he's using it for himself."

"No one can take Jimmy's place. Not really. You know that."

"I miss him a lot."

"I know you do."

When I was waiting for Jimmy to pick me up on North Wells that night, part of me had known something was wrong, something serious. I was scared on the way to the hospital and scared as we hurried through the halls, but here's the funny part: As soon as we turned a corner and I saw my aunt telling Mrs. Woolf Jimmy was dead, I stopped feeling scared. I stopped feeling anything at all.

"It's like I'm picking up all the feelings I left behind the night Jimmy was killed," I said.

"Well. You protected yourself from the hurt for as long as you could. Until you were ready to face it. Until now."

"This is more than I thought I'd have to go through."

"You're worn out," my aunt said. She brushed some hair away from my face. "Let's go home, okay? I'll call Fay later and tell her you're spending the night."

"It's okay?" I said. "You don't have other plans?"

She gave me a hug. "Not a thing. Come on. Let's go home."

At home I changed into a plum-colored sweatshirt of my aunt's and a pair of her shorts. I tossed my wet clothes into the dryer, turned it on, and stared at the dryer window. I watched Jimmy's jacket tumbling around and around. The metal of the zipper kept clanking against the metal of the dryer walls.

"There you are," my aunt said. "I made up the bed in the guest room; why don't you lie down for a while— try to get some rest."

"I don't know." I turned and looked at her. "Do you think you'll have to go out? What if a patient calls or something?"

"I wouldn't just sneak off without letting you know. I'll be here when you wake up."

"I know I'm being a real pain in the ass, but I can't help it. I just want to know someone's around. I mean . . . I guess I need you."

"What's wrong with that?"

"I'm almost eighteen. I'm supposed to be an adult."

She smiled. "Adults don't need other people?"

"You know what I mean."

"I know you're exhausted. Come on." She took my hand. "Let's go upstairs. You look like you're about ready to collapse."

*   *   *

I kicked off my shoes and fell into bed. My aunt pulled the quilt up around me, then leaned back into the chair next to the bed. She tucked one foot under her and lit a cigarette.

"Am I screwing up your whole weekend?" I asked. "Who were you having lunch with when I called you at the restaurant? Dr. Petrie?"

"No . . . Dan and I aren't seeing each other anymore."

"You're not? When did that happen?"

"A few weeks ago."

"But I liked him! I thought maybe you guys'd get married and live happily ever after and all the rest of that stuff."

"Hmm . . . it doesn't always work out that way."

"God, everything's changing. You and Dr. Petrie . . . the Woolfs are moving and Jimmy's gone. . . . I guess *I've* changed too, and it scares me. I feel like I started out on a long trip when Jimmy was killed and I just kept getting farther and farther away from myself."

"Where are you now?"

"I don't know. On my way back, I guess."

"Maybe the trip's finally coming to an end, then."

"Maybe."

"I think grief has to travel a certain route, honey. If you could plot it out on a map, you'd probably have a line that twists and weaves and eventually ends up near the point of departure."

"I don't think I'm there yet. I still have a way to go."

"That's all right. You're doing fine."

"You think I'll be able to work all this stuff out?"

"I'm sure of it. Close your eyes now; you really look wiped out."

I closed my eyes. I could hear the dryer downstairs, tossing my clothes around in a rhythmic hum.

"I got so I could *feel* Jimmy's death," I said. "Now just tell me something: When does it stop hurting?"

I felt her hand close around mine. "Oh, honey— that," she said, "is the million-dollar question."

31

Maybe in the night the first healing began, I don't know. I only know that when my aunt woke me up the next morning, I knew I was going to be okay. My best friend had been killed and the sadness was there, but at the same time and for the first time I knew I was going to be okay. I really was.

"You look rested," my aunt said. She put her hand on my face. "How do you feel?"

"I don't know. I'm not awake yet."

"I'll let you go back to sleep in a minute. I'm going out on a house call, and I wanted you to know—"

I closed my eyes. "When'll you be back?"

"It may take a while. Why don't you meet me at Field's around noon, all right? We'll have lunch."

"Field's," I said. "Noon."

"The Walnut Room."

"Uh-huh." I rolled over onto my side and pulled the covers over my head.

"The *Walnut Room*. Did it register?"

"Yeah, I heard you," I said. "The Walnut Room."

* * *

Later in the morning, when I finally woke up and was really conscious, I got dressed and took a cab over to Jimmy's dance school and tracked down the registrar in an upstairs office.

"I was a friend of Jimmy Woolf's," I said. "I know the scholarship's already been given, but I want to make a contribution anyway. Maybe for next year or however you want to use it."

There aren't too many people who are going to argue with a cash contribution, and this woman was no exception. She thanked me and gave me a receipt, and I walked out of that school feeling pretty terrific, like I'd finally closed the book on something, like I'd finally done something for Jimmy, or maybe I'd only done it for myself. It didn't matter. It made *me* feel good, and that would have made Jimmy happy. I walked over to State Street and into Marshall Field's, past the counter where Jimmy had bought me my first pair of earrings. I took the elevator up to the Walnut Room and got a table for my aunt and me. It wasn't too long before I felt a familiar tug on my hair.

"Hi there," she said.

"How was your house call?"

"I need some aspirin."

"That bad, huh? I'll tell you a secret. When I'm sick and you drive out to take care of me, I always pretend I'm the only person you'll go on a house call for."

My aunt smiled. She dumped her purse and medical

bag onto the empty chair next to me. "I'll tell *you* a secret," she whispered. "You're the only house call I ever look forward to."

She signaled the waitress, who came and took our order for lunch: French dip, salad, fries.

"Guess what?" I said. "I think I'm going to be okay."

My aunt nodded and looked at me: a clear, even gaze. I had never seen her look so serious. "That's quite a discovery to make about yourself."

"I had to choose between Jimmy and me . . . and I picked me. That's what you were trying to get me to see yesterday, isn't it?"

"You couldn't get on with your own life, honey, until you let go of his."

"I know that now." My eyes filled with tears. "I guess you weren't kidding when you said it was going to hurt."

"It's going to take a little while."

"I'm still afraid. Afraid to like someone that much again. I guess I'll have to work on that. I mean, I'm glad Jimmy was a part of my life, and I don't want to close myself off from other people like him."

"Knowing what you have to lose, but risking the loss anyway," my aunt said. "That's what it's all about." She took a little gift-wrapped package out of her jacket pocket and handed it to me. "Happy birthday."

"I forgot! I forgot all about my birthday!" I tore the paper off the package and opened it. Inside was a silver necklace with a tiny diamond flower dangling from it.

"This is really beautiful. Thank you." I fastened it around my neck. "How does it look?"

"Pretty. Like you." She reached over and opened her medical bag and took out a pack of Tareytons that was lying right next to her stethoscope.

"I don't *believe* this! You even carry them around in your medical bag! Aunt Lo, come on . . . it really bothers me when you smoke."

She stared at the pack of cigarettes for a second, then put it down in the ashtray. "All right, honey, okay. You're right. This is as good a time as any to stop."

"Really?"

"Mm-hmm." She took her lighter out of her purse and put it next to the Tareytons. "There."

"Good," I said.

We were halfway through the French dip when this ear-blasting beep started coming from my aunt's pocket. I concentrated on my sandwich and tried not to notice the entire restaurant staring at us like we were aliens receiving a coded message from our home planet.

"That's a really embarrassing piece of equipment you've got there," I said.

"There are worse places it can start beeping, honey, believe me." She pulled the pager out of her pocket and snapped it off. "Something tells me I better go find a phone."

She wasn't gone too long. A minute or two at the most. When she came back, she didn't sit down. She picked up her purse and her medical bag.

"Don't tell me," I said. "An emergency?"

"I'm sorry, honey. I have to go."

"That's okay. I guess someone else needs you now." She pulled some cash out of her wallet and put it beside the check for our lunch. "What train are you catching home? Do you need cab fare to the station?"

"No, I'm okay. Anyway, it's kind of nice out. I think I'll walk." I took a last bite from my French dip and stood up. "Wait a second; I'll ride down with you."

There were a lot of things I wanted to tell my aunt and not enough time to tell them in. Before I knew it, the elevator ride was over and we had stepped into a crowd of shoppers.

"There's something I have to tell you." I practically had to shout, but she stopped and looked at me intently, like I was the only other person in the store. "I just wanted to thank you . . . for giving me back myself."

"You're the one who did it, honey. All I did was point you in the right direction."

"I don't know. I think maybe you did more than just point me in the right direction. I think maybe you dragged me there."

And then there was that great smile. "You don't think you can get away without a hug, do you?" She put her arms around me and held me tight for a minute. "You're going to be okay," she said. "You know that now."

"Yeah," I said. "I know it."

"Call me tonight; let me know you got home okay."

"I will. 'Bye."

I turned around and walked out of Marshall Field's and onto State Street. I thought about the emergency she was rushing to: I had no idea what the problem was or who the patient was. I only knew that someone was in bad shape somewhere and maybe their first connection with something good would be when my aunt came into their life. And that person would be damn lucky, because they'd be in good hands.

I walked down Madison and stopped on the bridge over the Chicago River. I remembered the Saint Patrick's Day a couple of years earlier, when Jimmy and I had stood on the bridge and watched them dye the river bright green. *"Hang in there, kid,"* Jimmy had said to me that day. *"Spring is just around the corner."*

Hey, Jimmy, I thought, *spring is here now and I'm going to be okay. I really am.*

I unzipped Jimmy's jacket and took if off and hurled it over the railing.

Knowing what you have to lose, but risking the loss anyway. That's what it's all about.

I stayed at the railing long enough to watch a gust of wind catch Jimmy's jacket and send it whirling around and around in a downward spiral. Then I remembered my train, and I hurried to the station.